# Everything Falls Apart

## Nathan O'Hagan

## About the Author

Nathan grew up on Merseyside, and now lives in Northamptonshire with his wife and two children and works full time for the NHS. After spending most of his teens and twenties in various unsuccessful bands, Nathan eventually turned his hand to writing.

He regularly writes features and reviews for the online fanzine *God Is In The TV,* as well as *Sabotage Times* and *Clash Music.* He is also the co-founder of indie small publisher, Obliterati Press.

Twitter: @NathanOHagan
Website: nathanohagan.weebly.com

## Also by Nathan O'Hagan

The World Is (Not) A Cold Dead Place
Out Of The City
Purge

With thanks to M. W. Leeming.

Cover design by Rob Appleby.

# CONTENTS

# The Weight

There are things I remember, things I won't forget. I remember the scratch of Dad's beard as he kissed me goodnight, the way he used it to tickle my neck. I remember him throwing me up in the air as we played in the garden, the feeling of flying, then plummeting towards him, convinced he'd drop me, which he never did. The feeling in my stomach as it seemed to flip upside down as I was thrown skywards, sure I was going to be sick, but never wanting him to stop. I remember how strong he always seemed, how he would lift me effortlessly above his head, or walk around with me hanging off his back or his leg, like I was weightless to him. I won't forget how he would sing me to sleep at night. Always the same song, with the words changed a bit to fit my name into it. *"Take a load off, Annie, take a load for free. Take a load off Annie, take a load right off me."* I never knew what the song was actually called, or what the real lyrics were, and I didn't really care. It was my song. Mine and Dad's. The sound of his voice, singing softly in a way that was at odds with his usually gruff voice. That's something I'll never forget.

But I also remember the darkness. The way he'd snap at me for nothing. I remember creeping into his bedroom when he'd been in bed for days. He wasn't ill. My mum would tell me he was 'resting', but I didn't understand why he was so tired, if he hadn't been at work for weeks. I remember sneaking in, the room dark except for a thin shaft of light coming in through the gap in the curtains. I remember pulling the blanket back to look at him. He wasn't asleep, but didn't really seem like he was awake either. I remember how, when I looked him in the eyes, he didn't really seem to see me. I'll never forget how he just looked straight through me.

That was a pattern with Dad; joyous, loving and playful one day, irritable, distracted and lethargic the next. I'd compare my friends' dads with him, wondering if the way he was was normal. I quickly figured out that it wasn't. As far as I could tell, other dads didn't spend weeks in bed. My friends didn't get woken up late at night by the sound of their dad crying, or the sound of their mum screaming, *"What the hell's wrong with you?"*

There was the good stuff that only my dad did, though. Other dads didn't turn up at school and insist on taking their kids out of class so he could take them on a train ride to the beach. Other dads didn't organise football matches with every kid on the street, all of them against him and his daughter, matches we'd always win.

But other dads didn't disappear. They didn't leave the house one day and walk into the woods, to a tree where they'd hidden a rope. Other dads didn't do that, and leave a huge gap in their kid's lives and hearts that they could never fill.

I never heard our song after that day. Never sought it out, never chanced across it. In fact, I'd forgotten it even existed, wiped my mind clear of it, burying any memory of it deep down.

Today, though, it came on the radio. Driving along the motorway, heading home from work, the radio tuned to a station I don't usually even listen to. After the news headlines, there it was. Out of nowhere, I heard those opening bars, sucker punching me. And it all came flooding back; all those memories, all those feelings that I'd buried as deep as I could, so that I didn't have to think about him; the memory of him too much for me to cope with.

In an instant I lost it, lost control of my emotions, and my car. I swerved over to the hard shoulder, cutting across the lanes as horns blared at me. I reached for the volume control to turn it off, but found myself instead turning it up, turning it up as loud as it would go. Loud enough to drown out the sound of the traffic, and of my crying. I sang along, not the real words, but our words. I sang, I screamed and I cried until the song was over.

Not wanting to remember, not wanting to forget.

# *Thumbs Up*

Grant lent over the pub pool table and lined up his shot. He drew back the cue, but hesitated. He slowly edged it forward and nudged the white ball to the side. Although this slightly improved the angle of the shot, his primary motivation for doing this was to avoid the divot in front of the ball, caused by one of many ciggie burns to the baize. That was how old the table was; the smoking ban came in ten years ago, and the abundant burns on it predated that by many years. There were so many burns and scuffs on it, it looked more like a 1980's second division football pitch than a pool table. With the shot now re-angled to avoid the first and most prominent blemish, Grant drew the cue back again.

*

Greg sat near the back of the bus and tried to ignore the gang of school kids pissing about down the front. He watched the buildings flying by, counting the number of shops and pubs that had closed down since he was last here, which seemed roughly approximate to the number of pound and 99p shops that had sprung up in the same time. He lost count when one of the kids' phones blared out with some sort of music. It might have been hip-hop, or possibly grime.

"Oi!" Greg shouted. "Shouldn't you lot be in school?"

"Fuck off you old cunt!" one of them shouted.

"You nasty little bastard. I might be a cunt, but I'm not fucking old," he replied, though it was at least partially drowned out by the laughter.

He sat and seethed for the rest of the journey, as the kids unsubtly took the piss out of him, the music now blaring even louder. As he approached his stop he pressed the bell to alert the driver. Waiting until the bus had already stopped, he walked to the stairs, and when at the top, reached over and grabbed the offending phone, before jumping the full flight, landing almost at the door. Before the kids could even react he was running off the bus, as the door closed behind him, trapping the kids who were only now giving chase behind them, shouting and gesturing at him. He waved them away, bent over and stuck the phone down the back of his trousers, rubbing it against his arse crack.

*

He walked round the corner, past more defunct businesses on the last leg of the journey. He walked into The Crown and approached the bar. He didn't recognise the fella there, but was about to speak to him when he saw who he'd been looking for. Grant was bent over the pool table, saggy jeans hanging halfway down his skinny arse. Greg approached him silently, watched him readjust the position of the cue ball like the cheating cunt he was, and waited for him to take his shot. Just before he hit the white, Greg hoofed him as hard as he could up the arse. The cue flew out of Grant's hand as he screamed, and flew across the table, clattering onto the floor. He grabbed a pool ball off the table and span round, stopping as he realised whose head he was about to slam it into.

"Greg! Fuck me, man, what the fuck? When did you get out?"

"This very morning, mate. About ninety minutes ago, in fact."

"Shit! I didn't know, I thought you weren't out for a few months yet. Why didn't you tell me?"

"I wanted to surprise you."

"Well, you managed that. I wasn't expecting to get someone's toe up me fucking hole till at least lunch time. Come on, what are you drinking?"

"Well, we're in The Crown, so I'd say weak, pissy-tasting lager from pumps that haven't been cleaned since I went away."

"Right, two dirty piss pints it is then."

*

Two hours and several pints later, the two of them were sat at a small table, their half-drunk pints in front of them.

"Fucking hell mate," Greg said. "I'm flagging here. Haven't touched a drop in months, going straight to me fucking head."

"Oh yeah, didn't think of that." Grant nodded, not looking much better for wear himself.

"You got any whizz or anything?"

Grant rummaged in his pockets. He pulled out a small plastic bag of white-ish powder and threw it onto the table.

"There you go, little welcome home present."

Greg picked it up and headed towards the bogs.

"You can just do it here, Dave won't mind," Grant said, nodding towards the bloke behind the bar.

"I know, but I could do with a shit anyway."

*

Greg sat on the toilet, scooping the speed into his nostrils while simultaneously squeezing out a crap he'd been holding onto all morning, determined that his first bowel movement of the day would be as a free man. He finished the speed and fiddled with the phone he had stolen. As it was unlocked when he swiped it, he was able to change the lock code on his way to the pub, and now he perused his victim's social media accounts at will, whilst receiving regular angry texts from the lad's friends, threatening to track him down and kill him. Greg found the camera option and hit record, and filmed directly into the bowl as he leant back and pulled his legs up. Months of stodgy prison food had clogged his bowels up pretty badly, but the rank lager he'd been drinking all morning had now lubricated things up nicely, and he filmed as a resulting turd slithered its way out of his anus into the bowl. He posted the video to the owners' Facebook, Instagram, Twitter and Snapchat accounts, as well as sending it via WhatsApp to 'Mum'.

He walked back into the bar to see Grant talking to someone whose face he knew, but couldn't place straight away. As he finished fastening his belt, it hit him. He began to back his way towards the bogs again, but the man looked up and caught his eye for a second, looked away, then sharply back at him. He narrowed his eyes a bit and leant in to say something to Grant, who half turned his head towards Greg and nodded. The fella nodded back before leaving the pub, glancing back in Greg's direction as he passed through the door. Grant staggered back over with another couple of pints of pissy lager.

"Was that who I think it was?" Greg asked him

"I dunno. Depends who you think it was. If you think it was Gloria Gaynor, you're way off. If you think was Bryan, then you're spot on."

"Fuck me."

"What?" Grant asked, mopping up a spillage with a beer mat.

"What do you mean 'what'? Fucking Bryan?"

"Yeah?"

"Bryan, who works for Big Danny Wobba?"

Grant shrugged his shoulder as he sipped his pint.

"Big Danny Wobba who we owe money to?"

The look of confusion in Grant's eyes slowly turned to one of contemplation, to one of recognition, before, finally, to one of anxiety, all while continuing to sip from his pint.

"Oh right. Fuck. I'd forgotten about that."

"Clearly."

"Is it that big a deal? I mean, we don't owe him *that* much, do we?"

"Five grand."

Grant nearly choked on his lager.

"Five? Five fucking grand? How is that fucking much?"

"Well, let's just say Danny's rates of interest aren't as competitive as the average high street bank."

"Shit, man."

"And instead of repossessing your house, he takes possession of your fucking thumbs."

"Your fucking thumbs?" Grant nearly shouted, now even more anxious than his mate. "You fucking serious?"

"Well, he used to, but I don't know if he still does. He used to feed them to his shark."

"He's got a fucking shark?"

"Yeah, well he used to. Everyone knows that."

"I fucking didn't."

"That's where his nickname comes from."

"What nickname?"

"Wobba."

"That's a nickname?" Grant asked, seemingly becoming more confused as the conversation progressed. "I thought he was part German or Dutch or something."

"What? No, that's not his actual fucking name, you thick cunt. It's short for Wobbegong."

Grant didn't even reply this time, but stared right through Greg, who rubbed his face, growing as frustrated with this conversation as Grant was confused.

"Fuck me. Right, so Big Danny has a thing for exotic animals, right? He's got all these little bronze statues of… I dunno… alligators, fucking bears and shit. About ten years or so ago, somehow, he comes into possession of a tasselled wobbegong."

"Hang on," Grant said, slamming his almost-empty pint down, "am I supposed to have the faintest fucking clue what a fucking tasselled wobbegong is?"

"No, probably not. But it's a shark. It's one of those weird flat ones; it's got these fucking beardy things on the front. Ugly fucking things they are. They're mostly found round Australia I think."

"How *the fuck* did Danny end up with a fucking Australian shark?"

"Oh it was some fucking smuggler or something, I dunno, it's a long story. Probably."

"Alright then David Twatenborough, get on with the fucking story."

"Right, so when he gets it, it's just a baby, or a pup, whatever they call them, and the mad fucker thinks it's fully grown, so he keeps it in this old fashioned tin bathtub he kept in the warehouse. He fucking loved it, treated it like a baby, you know? But of course, it started growing, and before long it was filling the fucking bath, like. Couldn't even turn itself around. It was thrashing about, as though it was going mad, like those Russian bears they keep in tiny cages or something."

"So what did he do?" Grant asked, now gripped by the story.

"Well, after a week or two, Big Danny finally accepted that it was cruel to keep it like that. Broke his heart to admit it, but it was acting like it was going proper mental. I suppose Danny was mindful of the old lyric; 'If you love someone, set them free', so he decided he'd take it down to the docks in his van, and chuck it in there. He figured it was a shark, so it'd be fine in water."

"And was it?"

"Of course it fucking wasn't. It's from Australia, it's used to warm water. You ever been in the water down at the docks? It's fucking freezing. Even in summer. Plus it wouldn't have had anything to eat. I'm no wildlife expert but I reckon a shark needs more sustenance than some empty beer cans and used johnnies. It froze to death, probably within a few hours. The next day there was this big fucking shark floating on the surface, belly up. It was in the local rags. I guarantee, to this day, that'll remain the only ever sighting of a deceased tasselled wobbegong down at Bridge Street docks."

"Are you making this shit up?"

Greg held his hands up.

"I fucking swear. No word of a lie."

"Fucking hell."

"Yeah. So that's where the name comes from. But right now, I'm not worried about how he got his name as much as I'm worried about him taking our fucking thumbs."

"Oh I don't think it's gonna come to that. I mean, I've been walking around the whole time you've been inside, and nobody's come looking for me. And they all know where to find me," he said, gesturing around him, "I think you're blowing it out of proportion."

"I'm fucking not. The only reason he's left you alone is that the money was owed by both of us together."

"So?"

"He's got a weird sense of honour and principle. I promise you, if it'd just been you that owed it, you'd be struggling to hold that pint glass by now. If it was just me, he'd have had me done inside. He's been waiting for me to get out, all the while letting the interest accumulate."

"I still think you're getting a bit carried away. I'm sure we can reason with him."

"A man who keeps a fucking shark in a bath and removes thumbs? Yeah, you're probably right."

*

A couple of hours later the two of them staggered out of the pub. They had barely turned into Grant's street when a voice called their names. They turned around and Bryan was leaning out of his car window.

"Erm… alright Bry," Grant said.

"Alright," said Greg. Bryan didn't return the greeting.

"Danny wants to see you two," he said.

"Erm, we're a bit busy right now," Grant began, "can you tell him –"

"Now, lads," Bryan interrupted, "get in."

Greg and Grant looked at each other nervously, but complied.

*

They drove in silence, Greg next to Bryan, Grant in the back seat. They pulled up at an old warehouse close to the docks. Bryan got out and they followed him in. He closed the door behind them and they instantly spotted Big Danny in the corner, his back to them.

"Wait here a sec," Bryan said, and walked towards Danny. Grant turned to Greg.

"Right," he said, speaking quietly, "let me do the talking. I say we just brazen it out, be as chummy as possible, and see if we can work something out. I'm pretty friendly with Bryan, so that might help. Okay?"

"Worth a try I suppose," Greg said, shifting his weight from foot to foot.

"What you fidgeting for?"

"Fucking need a piss, man. That lager's been going through me."

"Just take it easy, it'll be fine. Just leave it to me."

"Alright fine. Don't mention the shark though."

"Why?"

"Apparently he's very sensitive about it. He's very sentimental for a mad, thumb-removing gangster type."

Bryan and Danny started approaching them. Greg followed as Grant approached them, arms out in a friendly gesture.

"Danny," he said as they met halfway, "how the hell have you –"

He didn't get to finish the sentence as Danny slammed his fist into Grant's face, sending him straight to the floor with blood pouring from his nose. Greg felt his bladder tightening, and his bowels loosening.

"Fucking hell," he said involuntarily.

"You fucking what, you little cunt?" Danny shouted.

"Nothing Dan, it's okay mate."

"It's not fucking okay. You fuckers owe me money. Eight fucking grand."

"Eight?" Grant managed to say through his fingers, as he tried to stem the flow of blood. "I thought it was five?"

"IT'S FUCKING EIGHT!" Danny yelled, kicking him in the guts.

Greg did a quick calculation in his head.

"Oh right, yeah. It is more like eight. My mistake."

"Both of your fucking mistakes. So where is it?"

"Danny, mate," Grant said, kneeling up. "We were on our way over to see you about that, honest mate. We were gonna come right over and sort it."

"Oh really? Oh well that's different then isn't it? Hear that, Bry? They were on their way over." He knelt down next to Grant. "So, where is it then? It doesn't look like you've got that sort of money in your pockets, and I'm afraid we're currently unable to accept cheques or debit cards."

"Well, the thing is, we haven't got it. Not right now. I mean, we thought we could work out some sort of payment plan."

Danny punched him in the face again. Greg's bladder strained inside him, and he let out a little groan of discomfort, mixed with one of fear.

"Of course we can work out a payment plan. The plan is, you fucking pay me. Now. Or..." he reached into his trouser pocket and took out a small silver item, which the boys couldn't quite see, "... I take your fucking thumbs."

Danny grabbed Grant's hand and shoved the thumb into what everyone now saw was a cigar cutter. He closed it until it was cutting into Grant's thumb. He screamed out, and Greg finally lost the war with his bladder, and felt his crotch and leg go warm as he pissed all over himself.

"No, please Danny!" Grant yelled. "I need me thumbs!"

"Don't!" was all Greg could manage to yelp, his embarrassment now equal to his fear.

"Fucking hell, Danny, look at this one," Bryan shouted, laughing. "He's fucking pissed himself."

Danny momentarily stopped what he was doing and looked over at the huge wet patch spreading over Greg's jeans.

"You fucking dirty bastard," he said.

"Please Danny," Grant said, using this unexpected lull to try and keep his opposable digit. "Don't do this. We must be able to sort something out. We'll do anything, Danny. Please."

"What could I possibly want from you two scuzzy little twats?"

"Actually, Dan," Bryan said, "there is something."

He beckoned Danny towards the corner, and Danny, seemingly intrigued, followed.

"And you two, fucking stay there."

Grant got back up to his feet, wiping the blood on his sleeve.

"You okay?" Greg asked.

"Not really. What about you?" he asked, gesturing at the piss marks.

"I've been better."

They watched Bryan and Danny confer in the far corner.

"Should we just fucking leg it?" Grant asked,

"Where've we got to run to?"

"Good point."

After a few minutes, Danny looked back towards them.

"Right, come here," he shouted.

Grant started walking towards him.

"And you too, pissy trousers," Danny shouted, and Greg followed.

"Okay, we've got an offer for you," Danny said, his foot up on an upturned crate.

"What offer?" Greg asked.

"Well, either I take your thumbs, or you do something for me."

"What would we have to do?"

"You two know Kev?"

"Kev Johnson?" they asked in unison.

"The very same. Well, Kev, like yourselves, owes me. But Kev's debt is... of a different nature to yours. It's the kind of debt that can't be covered by a couple of thumbs. Or any number of fingers for that matter."

"So where does that leave us?"

"Well Grant, Kev has pushed his luck one too many times with me, and he needs to go."

"Go where?" Greg asked with trepidation.

"Use you fucking imagination, lad."

"What?" Greg shouted. "You want us... you want us to kill Kev? Kill him? Us?"

"Seriously? Danny? Come on, I know we owe you, we can sort something, anything, but you can't expect us to –"

"I don't *expect* you to do anything. I'm just making you an offer. You know what the alternative is, so the choice is yours."

Grant looked at the mark on his thumb where the cigar cutter had begun to slice into the skin, and the blood on his sleeve. Greg looked down at his trousers, the front of them now entirely a few shades darker thanks to his lack of bladder control.

*

Greg passed the spliff back to Grant as they sat crossed legged on the floor of Grant's flat.

"Does he really deserve to die though?" Grant asked.

"Do we really deserve to lose our thumbs?"

"Well, we sort of do. In that we owe money to someone who's notorious for removing the thumbs of people who've wronged him."

"True. But are we prepared to lose them?"

"Clearly not, we've agreed to kill some poor fucker so that we don't."

"Poor fucker?" Greg spluttered. "Let's not stretch it mate. He probably doesn't deserve to die, but he's not some poor fucker. He's a fucking annoying prick, always was. If we don't kill him, then someone else will at some point, if not Danny."

"What's the best way to do it? I mean, obviously a gun would be best, but we can't get a gun, so what's the best option for us?" Grant asked.

"I dunno. We could poison him. Get a fuck load of rat poison and tell him –"

"What, tell him it's fucking sherbet?"

"No, we could make him something to eat, and put it inside."

"Yeah, coz us offering to bake him a fucking Victoria sponge won't make him suspicious will it?"

"Alright then, smart arse, what's your suggestion?" Greg said, taking the spliff back again.

"Fuck me, I dunno. We could push him in the fucking docks. In tribute to Danny's fucking wobbegong."

They sat in silence for a few minutes, their eyes occasionally flicking around the room as though on the lookout for some sort of murderous inspiration. Grant let out a big sigh.

"A hammer?" he said.

"You what?"

"We could use a hammer."

Greg weighed it up for a moment.

"A hammer is easily obtainable," Grant said. "In fact I've got one under the sink."

"Alright," Greg replied. "Fuck it. A hammer."

They waited on the corner, just down the road from The Crown. Grant held an off-licence bag full of cans of lager and bottles of cider.

"Right," he said, "so we're clear? We catch him on his way out, invite him back to mine, get him properly smashed, then properly smash his head in. Okay?"

"Whatever," Greg said without making eye contact.

"Oh what the fuck's up with you now?"

"Nothing."

"Are you still pissed off because you've gotta do it?"

"Well wouldn't you fucking be?" Greg said, turning to face him.

"Well yeah, but somebody's got to do it haven't they? And we agreed on scissor/paper/stone. We could have gone for the coin toss, but it was your choice."

"We should have done best of three."

"We DID do best of three!"

"Well, fucking best of five then!"

"Oh, fucking grow up, Greg. It was fair. Somebody had to lose."

"You should have offered to do it. As a gesture."

"Why?"

"Because I've just got out."

"That was fuck all to do with me, Greg. I didn't put you there."

"Alright, fine. I'll kill the fucker. I'm actually sort of looking forward to it now, the fucking trouble he's caused."

"Well, in a way, he's actually saved our thumbs."

"Suppose he has," Greg said. "Never thought about it like that. We owe him big. Still gonna kill the cunt though."

Moments later the cunt in question emerged from the pub, singing an Elbow song loudly to himself.

"Tell you what," Grant said, "if he doesn't stop singing that fucking shite, I'll kill him meself, right here."

They waited for him to approach, and turned the corner in time to bump straight into him.

"Alright lads," he said, adopting an arms-out stance. "You're out then Grant?"

"Yeah, I'm out, but I'm Greg, that's Grant."

"Yeah, yeah, yeah, sound. Sorry mate. Had a few, you know?"

"Yeah, no worries," Greg continued. "So, what you up to now?"

"Nothing much, like. Yourselves?"

"Just got a few cans and that," Grant said, lifting the bag up. "Fancy joining us?"

"Oh well, that's very generous of you lads. Very hospitable, like. I'd love to. Lead on, McDuff, lead on."

\*

Back in Grant's flat, Kev leaned over the side of the armchair, rifling through Grant's CD collection.

"Haven't you got any Stone Roses, mate?"

"Yeah, in there somewhere," he said. He looked over at Greg, who had barely said a word since they got there, and was now sat in the corner, staring at Kev and knocking back a can.

"Ah here we go, bit of Oasis, that'll do nicely," Kev said, placing the CD clumsily into the player. He skipped along a few tracks till the opening riff of 'What's The Story' blasted out. He turned up the volume and stood up, doing a lame approximation of a Gallagher swagger around the room. "Fuckin' tuuuuune!" he said over the music.

Grant caught Greg's eye. He gestured to Kev, whose eyes were now closed in rapturous celebration of the music. This was the time, clearly. Greg hesitated. Grant urged him on with his eyes, and hand gestures. Kev knocked over empty cans as he danced around the room. Greg finally stood up, and pulled the hammer from under his chair. He approached Kev from behind, Grant also getting out of his chair.

"*Need a little time to wake up, wake up,*" Kev sang atonally. Greg lifted the hammer above his head and approached Kev. He was now within clear striking distance; he just had to bring the hammer down. He held it in the air for what seemed like an eternity, Grant still silently encouraging him. But he lowered the hammer, leaving it hanging at his side, just as Kev turned round to face him and opened his eyes, looking straight at Greg. He looked down at the hammer hanging at Greg's side.

"Aye aye," he said, "what's the story, morning glory?"

Greg swung the hammer from low, catching Kev full in the temple. Kev put his hand to his head, pulled it away and looked at the blood on it, as some more of the red stuff trickled from his wound.

"No need for that, Greg," he said, as though his feelings were more hurt than his head. Greg swung again, but made weaker contact this time, the hammer glancing off Kev's head. This seemed to spur Kev into action. He grabbed Greg around the arms in a bear hug and lifted him up off the floor.

"This isn't how you play host," he shouted into Greg's ear.

"Fucking do something!" Greg managed to say to Grant as he struggled for breath. Grant, until now frozen to the spot, picked up a cider bottle and hit Kev on the back of the head with it. Being plastic, it simply bounced off and onto the floor. The impact seemed enough to distract Kev, though, who turned around to face him. Grant threw the kind of weak punch people throw when they're more scared than angry. Again, Kev looked more upset than hurt, or even angry.

"I'm gonna tell everyone what kind of parties you throw, you bastards."

Greg, who had now recovered his breath, hit him on the back of the head with the hammer. Kev turned to face him again.

"Look lads, can't we solve our differences amicably?" he asked.

"Fucking hit him again!" Grant shouted to Greg. Greg did as instructed. This time, Kev was knocked instantly unconscious, hitting his head on the corner of the table on the way down to the floor. This time, there was more than a trickle of blood from the head wound.

Grant quickly put a tea towel under his head to soak some of it up.

"Fucking hell," Greg said, sitting down, "that was harder than I expected."

"Is he dead then?" Grant said, also sitting down

"Fucking looks it to me," Greg said, still catching his breath.

"Aren't you gonna check?"

"*You* fucking check! I'm the one who fucking killed him, the least you can do is make sure."

"Alright, fine," Grant said. He walked gingerly over to the body. He bent over and looked at it. He nudged it with his foot. No movement. He nudged it a bit harder. Still nothing.

"Yeah," he said, "he's definitely dead."

"AAAAARRRRRRRGH!!!" Kev suddenly leapt up and rugby tackled Grant to the ground. "I'll teach you to invite me here under false pretences!" he shouted as he pinned Grant to the floor.

Greg was in action quickly, picking the hammer back up and swinging it into the back of Kev's head several times. It slowed him down, but didn't stop him, as he grabbed Grant around the throat and began to squeeze. Greg turned the hammer around and swung it, claw end first, with all that remained of his strength. It embedded in the top of Kev's skull. Greg tried to pull it out but it was stuck. Kev let go of Grant's throat and stood up, trying to pull the hammer out. He staggered around the room a while, his movements becoming slower and slower. Eventually, he sat down on the floor in the corner, no longer trying to remove the hammer. His breathing slowed and he stopped blinking.

"Fucking hell," Greg finally said after they'd stared in silence at him for several minutes. "Killing people is really fucking hard work. It's not like in movies. I'm fucking knackered."

"I'll bring the car round," Grant said.

Grant's Ford Ka was uninsured, had no M.O.T. and was barely road-worthy, but they didn't have the option of procuring another vehicle. They carried Kev out to the car. Grant, walking backwards holding the head end, struggled to get his keys from his pocket. Kev slipped from his grasp and hit the floor with a heavy thud.

"Oi!" The voice made both of them jump. They were surprised to see three teenagers emerge from behind a nearby hedge. Greg recognised at least one of them straight away.

"Where's me fucking phone, yer prick?" he asked Greg.

"Your fucking phone? Seriously?"

"Yeah," the teen said. "I've been fucking tracking it. There's an app on it, you thieving twat. Now fucking give it back." As he was talking, one of his friends looked down at the ground, and began tapping him on the arm. "Fucking what?"

His friend pointed to the body, its head on the floor, pouring with blood, its feet in the hands of the phone thief. The lad looked from Kev's mangled head, to Greg, to Grant and back to Kev's head.

"Keep the fucking phone mate," he said to Greg, before he and his friends legged it.

They bundled Kev onto the back seat and set off.

*

"Where is this place then?" Greg asked.

"Not that far. Maybe a twenty minute drive. We'll be off the motorway in a few minutes then it's really quiet roads after that, especially this time of night. It's just woodland where we're going. Nobody ever goes there. It's too out the way, even for dog walkers."

"Okay, sounds perfect."

Greg closed his eyes and let his head rest back against the seat as Grant drove. Grant blinked hard to keep his eyelids from closing.

"Frrrgnyr."

"You what?" Grant asked.

"I didn't say nothing," Greg replied.

"You were talking in your sleep."

"I wasn't asleep."

"Well then what was..?"

"AAAAAARRRRRRGH YA BASTARDS!"

Kev sprung from the back seat and grabbed them, an arm around each neck.

"Fucking hell, Kev!" Grant shouted. "I'm trying to drive here!"

Greg tried to throw his fist back to punch him, but the angles were against him and he couldn't reach. Grant swerved all over the road as Kev squeezed their necks harder. He slammed on the breaks, and Kev's grip finally gave way as he flew through the windscreen and landed with a horrid thump on the road, thirty yards in front of them.

"Jesus cunting Christ!" Grant shouted. "What is he, fucking Rasputin?"

"Why won't he fucking die?"

"Oh, he must be dead now. Surely? He went through the windscreen for fuck's sake."

Just as Greg spoke, the body began to shuffle on the ground. Slowly, Kev began to kneel up.

"Oh come on!"

Kev stood up unsteadily, looking around, as though trying to figure out his whereabouts.

"Just fucking die will ya Kev, for fuck's sake. This is fucking stupid now, mate."

Kev turned slowly round at the sound of Greg's voice. He squinted through the glassless space where the window used to be, raised his hand slowly, and, as though seeing Greg and Grant for the first time this evening, waved.

Grant revved the engine before driving as fast as the clapped out Ka could manage, straight into Kev. His battered body bounced off the bonnet and over the car, crashing down behind them. Grant hit the brakes, before reversing back over him, then drove forward over him once more, for good measure.

"Right!" he said. "If he's not fucking dead now, then I fucking give up. Danny can have me fucking thumbs for all I care. Maybe he'll let us keep one each, for at least trying."

"Maybe go back and forth over him once more?" Greg said. "You know, to be sure."

"Yeah, alright."

*

Twenty minutes later, they were standing in front of a large wire fence. 'Building site secured by Heritage Security' the sign on the fence read.

"Great. A fucking building site. Well that's just fucking perfect isn't it, Grant?"

"I didn't fucking know they were building here."

"And you didn't think to fucking check?"

"Obviously fucking not!"

"Brilliant, so what the fuck do we do now?"

"I don't fucking know, do I?"

"Fuck me!" Greg said, kicking the fence a few times.

"We'll have to get him back to mine."

"For fuck's sake. Yeah, I suppose you're right. Then what?"

"Fuck knows," Grant said. "We'll figure it out when we get there."

They walked the twenty yards back to where they'd left the car and got in. As they buckled their seat belts, Greg turned his head to the back seat and stared at it for a moment. He turned back to look out of where the windscreen used to be.

"Grant?"

"What is it?"

"He's gone."

"Eh?"

"I said he's gone."

"Of course he fucking is."

Greg didn't even bother turning round to check. At this point, nothing seemed out of the ordinary. They got out of the car, took the torch from the boot and began scouring the nearby woods, the building site, and the road for a mile in either direction. There was no sign of Kev, not even a trail of blood.

"This is getting a bit fucking supernatural now," Grant said.

"It's not fucking supernatural, it's just fucking annoying. He's taking the piss now."

They stopped walking and stood in the middle of the road.

"Look," Greg said, leaning over with his hands on his knees, "we've checked the roads, we've checked the building site. The only place the fucker could have gone is deeper into the woods than we checked. Right?"

"I dunno. Maybe, yeah."

"We're miles from anywhere. There's no fucking way he can survive the night. If he doesn't bleed to death, which he absolutely fucking has to, then the internal injuries will kill him. And if they don't, then he'll probably fucking freeze to death, or go into shock and just... fucking... die. Right? I mean he fucking *has* to!"

"I wouldn't be too fucking sure. Not after what he's already survived."

"Look, that was just some sort of freak occurrence. Maybe he's one of them freaks who can't feel pain. Yeah? And he's just taking longer coz the pain isn't registering or whatever. You know?"

"Yeah..."

"I say, we go back to yours, we go and see Danny in the morning and tell him it's done, and that we buried him in the woods, like we said we would. He doesn't need to know all the details, just that the cunt's dead. Agreed?"

"I suppose so. I just wanna go home, I'm fucking exhausted."

\*

The next morning, they paid a visit to Danny. No mention was made of Kev's superhuman levels of pain endurance, just that he had been dispatched and disposed off. Danny was satisfied, and the debt was written off.

\*

Despite the pressure being off, Grant and Greg decided to get out of town for a couple of days and stay with some of Greg's family in North Wales. Three nights after their visit to Danny, they arrived back at Grant's flat. As they entered the living room, Big Danny Wobbegong was sitting in the same armchair Kev had occupied. The door was shut behind them, and Bryan and another thick-necked associate of Danny's knocked them both to the floor.

"What the fuck? What's going on Danny?" Grant asked, with a mixture of fear and indignation.

"What's the matter? Ha, he's a funny cunt this one isn't he Bry? Did you forget our little deal, Grant? A certain person being got rid of, and you keeping certain parts of your anatomy?"

"What you on about?" Greg said, trying to stand but being kept in a kneeling position by the two goons. "We did what we said we were gonna do. We told you that. It was all taken care of."

"Oh, is that right? Well then why is it that Bryan saw our mate Kev in The Crown last night, with nothing more than a fucking bandage around his head, and a slight fucking limp?"

Grant and Greg looked each other. Danny reached into his pocket, pulled out his cigar cutter, and smiled at them.

"Thumbs up, lads."

# *Acts of Penance*

He had made his first million by the age of thirty. Inheriting his father's business when he was just twenty-seven, he displayed astuteness far beyond his years, and oversaw a swift expansion, opening up several more offices the same year and buying up dozens of rivals. By the age of forty, he was already a billionaire, the youngest in the country. Five years earlier, he had married his childhood sweetheart, and reaching billionaire status coincided with his son's fifth birthday. He celebrated these dual landmarks with an aggressive takeover of a high street sports retailer, followed by the purchase of a high-end supermarket. Pub chains, discount retailers and garden centres followed. By the time his daughter was born, he was the wealthiest man in the country.

*

She woke up at just after 7am, the sun shining in through the vast window of their bedroom. Her husband wasn't there. It wasn't uncommon to wake up this early and find him gone. When she did, she would usually head down to the kitchen, make him a coffee and take it through to his home office, where he will have been since as early as half-five, making and taking calls from America or Japan, checking share prices. A man didn't get to be this rich and powerful without having an intense work ethic, and, even in his late fifties, his work ethic was as intense as ever.

She got out of bed, put on her robe and walked downstairs to the kitchen. She switched on the Prima Donna ESAM 6600 coffee maker. When it had worked its magic, she picked up the newspapers from the doormat and carried them and the coffee through to the office. The second she opened the door, she screamed and dropped it all to the ground.

The heavy mahogany desk was overturned; his computer had been thrown across the room, its screen shattered. Papers were scattered over the floor, covering every inch of carpet, and the framed photographs of him with world leaders, celebrities and other businessmen that covered the walls had been smashed.

He was nowhere to be seen. The patio door was hanging open, some of the panes of thick glass cracked. She cautiously stepped through the door and into the garden of their 14-acre home. She looked around and, in the corner of the garden, crouched near a hedge, his back to her, was her husband. She screamed again, and ran over to him, her slippers soaking up the morning dew from the grass. When she got twenty yards away from him, she slowed down, afraid of what she was going to see. As she got closer, she was relieved to see his back moving up and down and to hear the heavy sound of his breathing.

"Darling," she said quietly, "are you alright?"

He didn't answer, so she moved tentatively to the side of him. He was staring at his hands, his mouth hanging open, a long line of drool dripping from it.

"What happened? Are you alright? The office..."

"It has to change," he said finally.

"What? What has to change?"

"Everything. Me, this..." He made a vague gesture to the grounds of his house, but kept staring at his hands.

"What are you talking about? What happened to your office? For God's sake, you scared me half to death. I thought... I thought something terrible had happened."

Her fear was now turning to anger.

"Terrible? No, not terrible, the opposite in fact." He finally put his hands down and focussed on his wife. He stood up and put his arm around her, leading her back towards the patio door. "Something extraordinary happened last night. I can't quite explain it, but it was wonderful."

"Wonderful? What are you on about? What the hell happened to your office?"

"My office?" He laughed. "Oh, don't worry about that; that doesn't matter anymore. Not now." He led her back through the detritus of the room. "Now listen, I've got a lot of work to be getting on with. This is all going to take a lot of planning."

"What? What's going to take a lot of planning? You're not making any sense."

"I can't explain it right now, but it'll all make sense soon enough. Now, do me a favour, get the lawyer on the phone, and have him come over in an hour, I'm going to need his help."

And without another word, he gently pushed his wife out of the door and closed it behind her. She heard the key turn in the lock. She banged on the door a few times, demanding to know what was happening, but he ignored her. After a few minutes, she gave up and went to phone the lawyer as she had been instructed.

Not only was he a lawyer, but also one of his closest friends and confidants. He had been working with him for over twenty years now. He was Godfather to their first-born, and was practically a member of the family. Besides his wife, the lawyer knew him better than anyone.

When he had received a call just before eight this morning, he had come straight over. She explained what had happened as best she could in her now almost hysterical state. The lawyer calmed her down and went and knocked on the office door. She was hurt that he was allowed in without hesitation while she had been ignored.

For over two hours he stayed in there while she fretted and debated with herself whether to ring the kids. In the end, she decided not to, not wishing to alarm them. When the lawyer finally emerged from the office, his face was ashen. He sat down at the breakfast bar in the kitchen and struggled to look her in the eye.

"Well?" she asked. "What did he say? What the bloody hell is going on? Is he alright?"

"I'm not sure. Physically he's fine."

"What the hell does that mean? Don't you start talking in riddles too."

"I mean... I don't know. Has he been under a lot of stress lately?"

"Stress? Of course he's been under stress, he's under constant stress, you know that. But he thrives on stress.

There's been nothing unusual until this morning. Why do you ask?"

"Because I think... I think he may have lost his mind."

"Lost his mind? Why? What did he say?"

"Well," he said, rubbing his face, "he has just given me very clear and very precise instructions on how to go about selling off all his companies, all his shares and assets and properties. Everything. He wants to sell everything, and donate every single penny to charity."

She sat in stunned silence for over a minute.

"Why?" she said finally. "Why does he want to do this?"

"I don't know. I didn't really understand it. Something about a... vision he had."

"A vision?"

"No, not a vision, that's not the word he used. 'Realisation', that was it. He said he'd had a realisation last night, and that things had to change. He said he had to 'redress the balance'. He said the only way he could do this was to give everything away."

"That's ridiculous."

"Like I said, he's lost his mind."

The two of them were startled by the door of the office suddenly bursting open. He ran out and headed straight for the stairs, his wife and his friend following closely behind him.

"Darling? What are you doing?"

He kept running until he reached the bedroom. By the time they caught up to him, he already had his suitcase open on the bed, and was shoving his suits into it.

"Where are you going?"

"Just into town."

"Town? Why are you packing all your clothes?"

"I'm just taking them to the charity shops."

"What? All of them?"

"Every last stitch."

"Darling, this is madness, you can't just give all your clothes away. What are you going to wear?"

He looked down at his pyjamas and slippers, and motioned towards them.

"These will do fine."

She looked to the lawyer for some support.

"Come on old son, you can't possibly think this is a good idea. I mean look, you're never going to fit all your clothes into one suitcase anyway."

"You're absolutely right," he said, stopping for a moment. "I'm going to need some bin bags."

\*

Some hours later, he returned to the house on foot. He was still wearing the pyjamas and slippers, which had been significantly worn down by the long walk back from town. He explained that while in town, he had sold the Jag to a used-car dealership and instantly cashed the cheque. He had then gathered together a large group of homeless people, and used the money to buy them all breakfast at a café.

"Well, I hope you enjoyed your meal," she said sarcastically.

"I didn't eat a bite."

"Why not?"

"Well, it hit me while we were in the café. The TV was on in there, and they were showing a report on the news from somewhere in Africa, some famine-hit zone. I looked at all those starving people, and I realised that I am no more deserving of sustenance than they are."

"What? So you're just not going to eat anymore? That's the stupidest thing I've ever heard. You're just going to let yourself starve?"

"No, I can't do that, not yet at least. There's too much work to be done. For the time being, I will allow myself water and a piece of bread a day. That will keep me alive, any more would be indulgence, and there's been far too much of that already."

She picked up the coffee cup she had been drinking from and threw it across the kitchen.

"You're fucking insane. You've lost your fucking mind! I've spoken to the kids. They think I should have you sectioned. Maybe they're right. That's another point. What about me and the kids? Did you think about us at all? You're giving away everything we have. I'll end up homeless. What about the kid's inheritance?"

"You and the kids don't have anything to worry about. I've taken care of it all. It's all built into my plans. I've set aside £1m for each of you."

"£1m? You're the richest man in the country. You're worth billions. Since this morning, you've already given away more than you've left for your entire family. One poxy million each?"

"A million pounds. It's far more than most people earn in a lifetime. The people that work in my stores, they'd have to work three lifetimes to get anywhere near that. A million pounds is more than enough for any human being to lead a very comfortable life and to look after the future of their children, as long as they aren't greedy or extravagant. You've got the house too, that's yours, all yours. From now on, I only need my office."

She stared at her husband, who looked dead ahead, making no eye contact. She began to cry.

"You bastard. You fucking bastard. Sod the people in your stores. Sod the homeless, sod the starving. What the hell are you doing? Suddenly growing a conscience? After all these years? If you want to perform some sort of penance, why not just pay your staff more? Buy the Big Issue. Donate more money to charity. Hold some fund raising dinners."

"It's not enough. I started off thinking like that, thinking of little things I could do, but it wasn't enough, so I thought of some bigger things I could do. It was still nowhere near enough. I quickly realised the only thing that could come close was to give it all away. Everything."

\*

By that evening, everything was in place. He had a bank of televisions set up against the wall in his office, each tuned to a different 24-hour news channel. He sat in front of it with a new laptop signed in to his bank account. Each time he saw a news story that highlighted an existing need, he instantly made a huge donation to an appropriate charity. In instances where individuals were in need, he emailed the lawyer with instructions to find the person and give them some money. Before long, he was the subject of news interest himself. Somehow, word had gotten out about what he was doing. He granted a single TV interview, explaining his actions. Within a few hours, people were flocking to his home from all over the country, all begging him for financial assistance. Despite the massive queue of people forming outside his home, he insisted on seeing them all. One by one, all manner of people with all manner of tales of woe and need sat at his feet and told him their story.

For the next few days, he listened to them all (between the hours of midday and three pm, so as not to miss too many news stories), with a chequebook open on his lap. Each time someone finished, he wrote them a cheque, the amount of which depended on the nature and size of the person's need, and how much he believed them. Even the ones he didn't believe received something. He figured that, even if their story wasn't true, to have gone to the effort of coming here, their need must still be greater than his.

As the days passed and turned into weeks, he didn't set foot outside his office. He barely slept at all, only nodding off occasionally, before rousing himself and getting straight back to work. He watched the numbers drop from his bank balance. Even after all this time, there was still a fortune in there. He increased his donations, and the frequency of them. He set up standing orders to go out daily on top of all the daily payments he was making. Unicef, NSPCC, RSPCA, Greenpeace, WSPA, Oxfam, Red Cross, Poverty Aid

International, Amnesty International, Child Brain Injury Trust, the Human Rights Defence Council. All of them received huge one-off donations, and daily standing orders. He didn't leave his chair, let alone his office. He developed pressure injuries, which became infected as he soiled himself, but he refused to allow his wife to send for a doctor. The weight fell off him. He had stuck to his pledge to eat only a piece of bread a day, and some days refused even that. His face was gaunt and sunken. His once fleshy torso was flat, the ribs starting to poke through the skin. His fingers looked like pencils as they hit the buttons of his laptop. His daughter flew back from Hong Kong to be with him, but after taking a single look, couldn't bear to be near him. His son tried every possible method of persuasion to get his father to desist, eventually breaking down in tears when nothing worked. Again, he threatened to have him sectioned, his mother coming into the room to show her support.

"Isn't it funny," he said, his voice weak and croaking, "for the majority of my life I have lived in opulence while millions slept on the streets. I ate the finest foods while children starved to death. I wore the most expensive clothes while children in my own country wore tattered rags to school. I made my fortune exploiting my workers, engaging in shady, sometimes illegal business practices. By the age most people are having their first legal drink, I was already set for life. But it wasn't enough. I wanted more. I kept on and on, making more and more money, buying more and more things; cars, gadgets, houses. Jesus Christ, I own seven properties that I visit barely once a year. I had all this, and I was never satisfied. I lived that way, and no one ever questioned it. And now, when I finally decide to do something about it, to redress the balance, now you call me mad."

His son stormed out, saying, whatever happened, he didn't want to see his father again. Only his wife remained now. She too left the office, not in anger, but in resignation. She walked into the kitchen and poured herself a glass of wine. She drank it straight down and poured herself another. She realised now that protest was pointless. Whatever action she took now was delaying the inevitable. Whatever had happened to him that night, whatever he had seen that had set him on this path, there was clearly no stopping him.

*

A few nights later, she stepped back into the office and walked over to her husband, or what was left of him. The stench was unbearable. He was now little more than a barely living skeleton; a thin, almost translucent layer of skin stretched over the bones. A single thin finger tapped weakly at the laptop keys, as the pale eyes remained fixed on the bank of TVs. She knelt down next to his chair.

"Darling," she said quietly. He turned his head slowly towards her and tried to smile. Slowly, wearily, he lifted his free hand towards her face. He rubbed a bony finger over her cheekbone, and she leant her face into his feeble touch. It had taken all his strength to do it, and he let his hand drop back to the arm of his chair. His other active finger resumed tapping away at the keyboard. Despite the smell, she placed her head on his arm, closed her eyes, and went to sleep.

*

She had no idea how long she had been asleep. It wasn't a sound that had woken her, but the lack of it. The background hum of several different rolling news channels was still present, but the gentle tapping of the keys was now absent. She pushed herself back onto her knees and looked at her husband's motionless face. She pressed her ear against his chest. She could feel his sternum, every single rib, but felt no heartbeat. She wiped the tears away from her eyes and kissed his face; the forehead, the protruding cheekbones, the dry cold lips. She looked down at the laptop, still logged into the bank account that, though vastly depleted, was not empty. She lifted it from his thighs, sat down on the floor and placed it on her own lap. She looked up at the screens; the scenes of famine, floods, earthquakes, poverty, destruction, sorrow and neglect, and she understood. She began tapping away at the keys, as the TV images reflected in her husband's lifeless eyes.

# The Price of Banter

Tony placed his Tupperware box on the fridge shelf. It was just big enough to contain his cheese sandwich. On the left of the box he placed a single apple, and to the right a carton of Ribena. This was the same lunch he had brought to the office every day for seven years. Before that, he had experimented with a variety of different lunches, but had found that this one was the one that struck a perfect balance between being enough to keep him going until the end of the day, but not so much that he would feel overfull and sluggish for the afternoon.

He placed it all on the shelf exactly in the middle of the fridge. Again, having established the perfect lunch, he had experimented with every different shelf in there before settling on the third one from the top as the most suitable. Any lower, his sandwich became disconcertingly floppy. Any higher, his apple was too crisp. Interestingly enough, he had found that his Ribena had a one-shelf margin of error, and was just as satisfying on the second one from the top, or the third one from the bottom. However, it just made perfect sense to keep them all neatly contained together, on the same shelf. He clapped his hands together twice.

"Right then," he said aloud, to nobody in particular, "time to get to work."

"He does that every day, doesn't he?" Keith asked. He was watching Tony from across the accounts office.

"What's that?" Mike responded, distracted.

"That Tony one, he does the same thing every morning doesn't he?"

"Hmmmm?"

"He brings his lunch in in the same little plastic box, puts it on the same shelf in the fridge, with a drink and an apple either side."

"Yeah, creature of habit, I suppose," Mike said.

"And then he claps and says *'time to get to work'* to himself."

Keith did an impression of Tony's distinctively nasal voice when he quoted him, something Mike thought was unnecessarily mean-spirited. He looked up from his work for the first time in the conversation.

"He's harmless. He just likes things a certain way."

"Oh yeah, yeah. Don't mean no offence, like. Just funny. Wonder what he'd do if the shelf was taken."

"Well, we all tend to keep that shelf clear for him. It's sort of unofficially his shelf."

"Ahhh," Keith said. He was already formulating something. Just a little office prank. Keith prided himself on his office-based banter. The way he saw it, working in finance, everyone needed a bit of light relief from the drudgery of the job, and he was the perfect guy to provide it. He was just naturally funny in a way that most people weren't. The last place he worked in, everyone called him 'The Banter King.' Some of the stuff he used to pull there was absolute quality. Had everyone in stitches, he did. Cracking bunch of lads.

It was a bit different here, though. He quickly realized this when he started a few weeks back. Everyone was a bit more serious, like. Very focused on their work. Which was fine; Keith was very task-orientated too, but you can't take life too seriously. Keith had learned that the hard way. After beating testicular cancer, and the breakdown that followed, five years ago, he vowed never to take anything too seriously again, and to spread as much laughter as he could in the short time we've all got available. And this place definitely needed some laughter.

*

Tony's watch beeped twice, telling him it was now exactly midday.

"Right," he said, "time for a spot of lunch."

He put his computer into hibernation mode, and typed in the code on his phone that would switch on his voice message in case anyone rang.

*Hello, this is Tony,* the message said. *I am currently on lunch, but I will be back at my desk at precisely twelve thirty. Please call back then, or if you leave a short message, I will return your call as the first opportunity. Thank you.*

He walked over to the fridge and opened it. As he reached out toward his shelf, though, he stopped dead.

"Erm..." he said, though nobody was in the immediate vicinity. Still his hand was frozen in mid-air,

55

in front of the shelf. He closed the door, then immediately opened it again, as though this might change what he had seen. But it didn't. He closed the door again and turned towards the rest of the office.

"Excuse me, did anyone... has anyone... erm..."

"What's up, Tony?" Karen asked from her desk.

"Well, I was just wondering, did anybody happen to move my Ribena down to the next shelf for some reason?"

A low chorus of 'not me, mate's and 'no, Tony's passed across the office.

"Ahh," he said. "Hmmm."

"Maybe you put it there by mistake?"

Everyone turned to look at Keith, his head sticking up from behind his computer.

"No, no, I definitely didn't do that."

"You sure?"

"Yes, yes I'm very sure, Keith."

"Oh right. Maybe it moved itself then, Tony?"

"Moved itself? I'm not sure what you mean, Keith."

"I dunno, maybe it didn't like that shelf or something? Or maybe it saw a bottle of Oasis it liked the look of and wanted to get closer to it?"

"Erm, Keith, did you happen to move my Ribena?"

"Yeah, you got me, mate. Just a little office prank. No harm intended."

"Right, yes. Well, I'd really rather you didn't do that in future, Keith."

"No worries mate. Enjoy your lunch."

*

Keith watched Tony take his lunch from the fridge and go to eat it in the lunch room. He turned to Mike.

"Oh that was classic stuff. Did you see that?"

"Yeah, I saw it."

"Quality stuff, eh?"

"Actually, I didn't think it was that funny to be honest."

"What? You're kidding me? That was top-notch stuff that, mate. And I'm just warming up!"

"Warming up?"

"Yeah! The Banter King is back on his throne."

"Who's the Banter King?"

"I am, Mikey boy. And this is my throne," he said, gesturing to his chair.

"Right, okay. Well, I don't think it's a good idea to wind Tony up like that. He's sensitive. Just leave it now, yeah?"

"Oh, Mike. You won't be saying that when you see what I've got in store."

**THURSDAY**

*'Beep beep.'*

Lunch o'clock.

Tony approached the fridge with an odd sense of trepidation he couldn't quite explain. Keith's 'prank' yesterday had left him a little shaken, and he experienced some anxiety on the way into work this morning for the first time in years. Sure that such feelings were unfounded, he opened the fridge door.

"No," he said, a little louder than he'd meant to. In fact, he hasn't meant to say it at all; it was just a natural reaction. Today, the Ribena was back on the correct shelf, but his sandwich had been moved up a level, and his apple down a level. Given that his Ribena could withstand a one-shelf move in either direction, this was much worse. Has sandwich would now be a touch too cold, while his apple would be minutely too warm. Hardly any difference, really, but Tony would know.

"Keith!" Tony called out. "What have you done?"

"OFFICE PRANK!" Keith shouted, appearing from the side of the fridge. Tony jumped up.

"You've moved my lunch again, haven't you, Keith?"

"What makes you think it was me?"

"Well, erm, the evidence does suggest... I mean... you did say office pra –"

"Of course it was me, Tone. Just messing with you, my mate. Just having a laugh, you know? Trying to liven the place up a bit."

"This isn't really livening things up for me, Keith. This is causing me some distress."

"Like the Jamaican fella who goes to the fancy dress party? You know, where he has to go as an emotion, but turns up in a dress. You know that one, right?"

"I don't know what you mean, Keith. But please will you stop –"

"And someone says, *'What are you supposed to be? You're supposed to be an emotion.'* And the Jamaican fella, he goes *'I am... I am in dis dress.'* Eh? You having that one, mate?"

Keith even adopts a Jamaican accent that makes the whole office wince at the punch line.

"Look, Keith –"

"Yeah, yeah. I'm with you, mate. No more office pranks on your lunch."

Keith walked back to his desk. Mike leaned across to him.

"I thought I told you not to do that anymore? It's really not funny, you know."

Karen poked her head round the side of her computer. "You really need to stop this, Keith. It's akin bullying now."

Bullying? Keith couldn't believe his ears. The last thing he was was a bully. He was just having a laugh, and he knew what was funny. He'd grown up on 'The Two Ronnies' and Python, he wasn't about to take lessons on comedy from a couple of office drones.

"Oh don't be daft, Karen. It's not bullying, it's just banter. I'm just having a laugh"

"Yes, *you* are having a laugh, but Tony isn't, and nobody else is. When you're laughing *at* someone else, it's bullying. Now stop it, or I'll have to get HR involved."

"I'm going for a fag," Keith said, storming away from his desk. He saw Tony eating his sandwich, staring at the wall in the lunch room. He thought about going and saying something, telling him it was just a joke. That he didn't mean anything by it, but he continued on his path out of the door to the smoking area.

*

Keith took the DVD out of the player. Ricky Gervais Live. One of his favourites. Gervais was one of the comedians he most related to. A bit edgy, a bit close to the bone, but ultimately harmless. That's what Keith's own humour was like, he thought. He liked that Dapper Laughs fella too, a bit naughty, maybe went a bit too far at times, but ultimately he was a good bloke. Keith still followed him on Twitter and shared his posts.

He decided to have one more can before bed, and turned the telly over to Dave. There was usually something good on there or UK Gold. Always a repeat of an old 'Only Fools And Horses' or 'Fawlty Towers'. Classic British comedy. There was an Alan Partridge on Dave. Keith turned over instantly. Not a fan. Just doesn't really work for him, and that Coogan fella's a bit up himself. Luckily, there was an episode of 'Not Going Out' on the other channel. That's more like it.

Keith sipped his can and thought about what had happened at work. That Karen was a bit out of order. Threatening to get HR involved? Totally over the top. And Mike wasn't much better. Some of these people really must have had a sense of humour bypass. Miserable so-and-so's.

He had decided to just put an end to the jokes. Sod them, they can all sit there with faces like smacked arses for all he cared. All he'd tried to do was inject a bit of fun into the atmosphere of the office. Well, if they didn't want that, then that was their loss.

But then, thanks to a scene in 'Not Going Out', a flash of inspiration came to him. He knew what to do. This one was bound to win them all over. Even Tony would see the funny side of this one, eventually. And what a way to end the week. Just when it seemed like he'd lost the entire office, he'd pull them all back onto his side in one great office prank, and send everyone off into the weekend on a high, and an understanding of what The Banter King was really about. He switched the telly off and poured the last of his can away. He was so giddy with excitement, he wanted to get to sleep as soon as possible.

**FRIDAY**

"Morning everyone," Keith shouted as he arrived at the office.

"Morning," came the subdued responses.

He looked over to the fridge. Tony was there, placing his lunch onto his shelf.

"Morning, Tony lad," he shouted.

Tony turned around slowly, after closing the door.

"Yes, good morning, Keith."

"Have a good day, mate," Keith shouted back. He clapped his hands twice. "Time to get to work, Tony."

"Keith," Karen said, quietly.

"What? Just being friendly."

*

The morning dragged as Keith clock-watched, desperate for lunch time to come. He tried to keep as busy as possible, just to speed the morning along. Eventually, as the clock reached ten to twelve, he got up from his desk, and went to put the plan into action.

*

Tony opened the fridge door, and let out a strangled little yelp as he looked inside. He slammed the door and walked over to Keith's desk.

"What have you done with it, Keith?"

"What's that, Tony?"

"My lunch, Keith. What have you done with my lunch?"

Karen, Mike and others stood up to see what was going on.

"Don't know what you're talking about, mate. I haven't touched it."

"Keith, this really isn't funny. I want my lunch back, please."

"Keith," Mike said, "come on mate, just give him his lunch back. This really isn't funny at all."

"No," Karen agreed, "this most certainly isn't funny. Where is Tony's lunch?"

Keith leaned back in his chair and spread his arms. "Maybe you left it at home?"

"I didn't leave it at home, Keith. I never leave it at home. You know I haven't left it at home. So where is it, please?"

"Tony, I really don't know, mate. Tell you what, though, there's a fella in the printer room that might know."

Tony was breathing heavily now, scratching nervously at the back of his hand.

"What have you done, Keith," Mike asked, seeing how upset Tony was becoming.

"Go and ask the fella in the printer room."

Karen stood up as Mike led Tony out of the office. She leaned over to Keith.

"I'm going to HR over this, mark my words."

As she followed Mike and Tony out, Keith opened his desk drawer and took his chance.

*

"There's nobody in here," Tony said as the three of them reached the printer room.

"Wait," Mike said, "look at that."

Karen and Tony followed his finger to a poster on the wall. It was a colour picture of Tony's lunch, inside the fridge,

'IT'S IN THE FRIDGE.'

The three of them walked back into the office where Keith was busy typing away at his keyboard. Once again, Tony opened the fridge door. Slowly this time, afraid to see what was, or wasn't inside. As he did open it though, he saw, sure enough, on the correct shelf, his lunch. Just where he'd left it. Sandwich in the middle, Ribena on one side, apple on the other, just as they always were.

"Oh," Tony said, scratching more vigorously at the back of his hand "it's all there. But it wasn't there. I assure you, it wasn't there."

Mike put a reassuring hand on his shoulder. "I know, Tony. That bloody Keith."

"Yes. Keith. Bloody Keith," Tony said, breathing more heavily.

"I'm going straight to HR over this, Tony," Karen assured him.

"Bloody Keith," Tony repeated, his voice raising. "Bloody Keith."

"It's okay, Tony. I'll speak to HR, and to Gordon, and make sure he doesn't do this again."

Tony wasn't listening anymore, though. He was staring at his apple, his eyes narrowing and his head turning to the side, trying to take something in. He reached into the fridge and took it out. He lifted it up to eye level, and turned it slowly around, to reveal a huge bite taken out of it.

"Oh my God," Mike said.

"BLOODY KEITH!"

Tony's shout took Mike and Karen by surprise, and they failed to react when he took his Ribena out, and carried, along with his apple, over to Keith's desk.

"Alright there, Tony?"

Tony placed his apple on Keith's desk, the bite facing towards him.

"Ooh, no thanks, mate. I've already eaten."

"Keith?"

"Yes Tony?"

"Office prank."

Before Keith could speak, Tony held his Ribena against his head, and brought his other hand down on it, bursting it all over Keith's face and shirt.

"What the fuck, Tony?"

"OFFICE PRANK!"

Tony picked up the apple, and held it high above his head.

"No need for this, Tony, it was only –"

"Yes, Keith, an office prank. Well, so's this!"

Tony shoved his hand into Keith's mouth, forcing his lower jaw open, and pushed the apple in with the other hand. Keith struggled, and it was a tight fit, but Tony's rage had given him superhuman strength, and he managed to force it past Keith's teeth, where it lodged inside his mouth.

By now, the rest of the office, previously too stunned to react, had come back to life, and a few hands tried to restrain Tony. But whether his rage was too much for them to contain, or whether, deep down, they thought Keith deserved all he got, and thus their hearts weren't really in it, their efforts were in vain.

Keith's garbled, apple-muffled protestations went unheeded as Tony took the stapler from his desk and lifted Keith's tie to his forehead.

"OFFICE PRANK!" he yelled as he stapled Keith's tie to his head.

"OFFICE PRANK! OFFICE PRANK!" as he punched in staple after staple.

The sight of blood trickling down Keith's forehead was enough to prompt his co-workers to finally drag Tony off him.

"Easy, Tony, easy there mate," they said soothingly as they held him back.

Keith fell to the floor, breathing through his nose as he tried to dislodge the apple, whimpering as he tried to unstaple his tie.

The Banter King, forever dethroned.

# Fucked Up

Friday Night. Friday night is fanny night. Fanny Friday. The cunt hunt. The pussy patrol. The minge mission. The snatch snare. Every Friday is the same. Me and my mates, we like to call ourselves the cunt crew. The twat team. The gash gang. The bush bashers. The fanny finders.

I'm a fanny rat. Always have been. As long as I can remember, anyway. I love to fuck. No, that's not right. I *live* to fuck. It's what I look forward to all week. It's the only thing that keeps me sane while I'm doing my mindless, boring fucking job, knowing that eventually it'll be Friday, and the weekend will begin. In fact, it's not the weekend. As far as I'm concerned, Friday to Sunday *is* the week. The rest of it is a write off. It's a preamble, a prelude, a prefix to the real thing. It's the foreplay before the fucking. And fucking is what it's all about. Some gangs of lads, it's all about the fighting. Some, it's all about the drinking; some are all about the drugs. And these things are all great, but for me and my mates, they would be nothing without getting your end away.

Work finishes at five and we head straight over to the boozer across the road. We neck a couple of pints, just to get the juices flowing. Then drive home and jump in the shower. I stick some tunes on and do a few quick reps with my weights and a set of push-ups so I'm looking as buff as possible. I put one of my good shirts on, a splash of Calvin Klein, fix my hair, then a quick line of beak, and a taxi into town.

We meet up in the Yates' or the Parrot and get some beers and a few sambucas down our necks, and it's on to the club up the road where all the fanny hangs out, and the cunt hunt begins in earnest.

Now, I know most gangs of lads out on a Friday probably talk like this. They're after the same thing we are, but we all have a 100% strike rate. The main factor in pulling isn't how good looking you are, or even how much you happen to possess the gift of the gab. It's all about choosing your targets carefully. You don't wanna be wasting valuable hunting time chatting to some stuck-up, drop-dead gorgeous model wannabe out to grab herself a Premier League footballer. If you haven't got a six-figure weekly income, these bitches don't wanna know you. And even if you did get one of them into the sack, chances are they're gonna be so up themselves that they just lie there and make you do all the work. And you can forget about them taking it up the arse or doing anything dirty. But at the same time, you don't wanna get some fat ugly bird just because you know she'll be easy and so grateful she'll let you do anything. No, you wanna save those for Saturday night (of which, more later).

Friday night, you wanna strike the balance just right. She doesn't have to be stunning, but she's gotta have something going on in the looks department. You want at least a 6 or 7 out of 10. With that basic standard having been established, then it's a case of ticking one or more of the other requirements.

Is she drunk enough? Again, you've gotta pitch it just right. You don't wanna pick some bird who's gonna throw up a whole night's worth of brightly coloured cocktails all over your dick, but she's gotta be drunk enough that her inhibitions are sufficiently lowered. Once these criteria have been met, then it's all down to personal taste. For example, Kevo likes blondes with big tits. Sam likes black birds and Tommo likes them curvy. Me? I like them young.

Now, let me be clear. I'm not a fucking paedo. I'm not into kids, but, on any given night, in any given nightclub in any given town or city, it would be naive to think that there aren't gonna be at least a few girls out and about who maybe aren't strictly the legal drinking age. And of those, there may or may not be a few who aren't quite the age of consent either. But shagging them absolutely does not make me a paedophile. Those fuckers are sick. They should all be sent to prison for life, and have their cock and balls cut off without anaesthetic. And I'd volunteer to do it as well.

The kind of girls I'm talking about, they aren't kids. If they're old enough to be out drinking, then they're old enough to be getting fucked. I bet every man in the land thinks the same way I do, the only difference is that I'm honest about it. And I don't see why me or anyone else should be embarrassed about liking a bit of tight young snatch. There's just nothing better than feeling a vice-like teen twat round your cock. There's also the extra safety with them. If you've got your cock in, say, a 17 year old pussy, then it's far less likely to be diseased than a 27 year old, isn't it? Which means you don't really even have to wear a condom with them (not that I generally wear them anyway, and even when I do I'll often take it off partway through without the girl noticing). They dress like sluts, they act like sluts, and they fucking drink like sluts. If they get past the bouncers, then, as far as I'm concerned, they're fair game. And am I expected to be checking the I.D. of every girl I fuck on the off-chance she's not legal? Fuck that shit. Go ahead; judge me if you like. I'm comfortable with my lifestyle. Clear conscience here, mate.

So that's what we like. That's what each of us is looking for on a Friday night. Of course, sometimes you just have to be willing to lower your standards a bit if your preferred type of bird isn't out in force. Once you get to the one o'clock mark, if you haven't already at least got your fingers wet, then it's time to rethink the plan, and consider grabbing anything that's willing. You don't wanna be going home alone. If you wake up alone on Saturday morning, then brother, you have failed miserably.

We all meet up for breakfast on Saturday morning, and you do not wanna be the only one to turn up without a smelly cock. Anyway, once we've discussed the nights previous events, and shared details of our conquests (much to the disgust of the bird who works in the cafe, but fuck her), talk will turn to Saturday night's plans.

Saturday night is what we call Sports Night. The difference being that, while you always want a bird of a decent standard on a Friday night, on Saturdays, we all agree the goals and targets for the night. It can be who gets to shag the ugliest bird, the fattest bitch, the oldest slag.

Tommo had us beat on the fatty front the other week. He went home with some absolute fucking heffer. She was fucking repulsive. The fact that he managed to get a hard on with her, and 12 pints down him, has earned him my unwavering respect and admiration. Not only that, but he also had the presence of mind, while he was banging away from behind at that repugnant fucking blob of a woman, to get his phone out and film it.

The sight of Tommo rutting away at that disgusting pile of human blubber while he gave her a mouthful of verbals is the funniest thing I've seen in a long time. You should have seen the fucking arse on this beast. In fact, if you look on the right websites, I'm pretty sure Tommo's put it online. Fair play to Tommo. He fucking smashed it out the park when it came to the fatties.

After a performance like that, it's necessary to raise the stakes, so we throw in a dare. Of late, that usually involves doing a shit somewhere in the bird's house, and leaving it there for her to discover the next morning. Or, in Tommo's case a few weeks back, leaving it in her bed for her to roll over into after he'd snuck out.

Kevo excelled himself the following week by leaving one in the girl's fridge, curled up on a china plate. But the best of all, if I do say so myself, was my effort last week. I was about to fall back on the old reliable shit-in-her-handbag trick, when I saw a hairdryer. In a flash of inspiration, I unscrewed it, and deposited a nice big thick turd in there, before carefully putting it back together. The only thing that took the shine off it a tiny bit was the fact that I couldn't be there to witness it the next time she switched it on.

That little act of genius was pretty much the full stop for the shit dares, so it's time to move on to something else. But what? Well, we'll decide that over breakfast. Before the bird in the cafe has refilled our coffees, we will have put it to the vote, and the games will begin.

# An Unexpected Encounter With A Minor Celebrity

Neil pulled into the car park of the Plaza Inn hotel on the outskirts of Ipswich, and shut his engine off. He caught a glimpse of himself in his rear-view mirror, and didn't like what he saw. His skin was pale and blotchy, his eyes had bags bigger than a pelican's beak pouch, and the only thing greyer than them was his thinning hair. He looked every one of his fifty-two years – the legacy of over two decades as a travelling rep. Driving up and down the country flogging office equipment, with working weeks of well over fifty hours having become the norm so long ago and so gradually that he hadn't even noticed it happen, and being away from home at least two nights every week, had taken its toll. He took his case from the boot of the Audi and wheeled it across the car park and into the hotel reception.

"Can I help you, sir?" the Romanian-sounding lad on the desk asked him.

"Yes, my company has booked me in here. Name's Moore."

The lad quickly tapped some keys on his computer.

"Ah, yes. Neil Moore. You're booked in for two nights, breakfast included. Will you be making use of our pool and spa facilities?"

"Erm, probably not, no."

"Are you sure? They're quite excellent, and no extra charge."

"No, I don't think so, mate. Cheers."

"Very well, you're in room 347, lifts are over there."

\*

He pushed his key card into the slot, and the room lit up. He'd never been here before, but he'd seen this room hundreds of times now. They were all basically identical in their layout, functionality and soullessness. Neil lay back on the admittedly very comfy bed and let out a sigh that had been building up for decades. He unpacked and hung up his spare suit, dumped his toiletry bag in the bathroom, and decided to head down to the bar for a drink.

\*

Sitting on a stool at the bar, Neil ordered himself a double Bushmills and ice, and turned around to see who else was in the bar. More specifically, to see if there were any women in there. Sleeping with other women when he was travelling wasn't something he made a huge habit of, but it wasn't unheard of. Over the years, he'd had maybe five hotel encounters with women, and even one with a man, where they'd wanked each other off while they watched porn on the other man's laptop. Tonight, there was only one woman in there, similar age, similarly melancholy disposition. She looked over at him and smiled. Neil was about to step off his barstool when his phone vibrated in his pocket. It was a message from Denise, saying goodnight. He put his phone away and downed his whiskey. *Not tonight,* he thought to himself, and left the bar.

The same young bloke was on the reception as Neil passed him and headed towards the lift. Having pressed the button to summon it, a thought occurred to him, and he walked back to reception.

"Erm, is the pool and spa still open, mate?"

"Yes sir, it's open twenty four hours. Just show your room key and you can use it at your leisure."

"Thing is, I haven't got any swimming trunks."

"That's alright, they are available for purchase in the pool area."

\*

Twenty minutes later, Neil was completing his fifth lap of the pool. He wondered why, in all the years he'd been staying in hotels, he'd never once used their swimming pools or gyms. It felt incredible, and he wished he'd done this every time he'd gone down to a hotel bar or ended up in the room of some equally lonely woman.

A few laps later, he heaved himself out of the pool, and lay on one of the sun loungers. He closed his eyes and began drifting off to sleep, but the sound of the door to the pool area opening woke him. He didn't open his eyes to look, but heard a loud splash as whoever it was seemingly jumped straight into the pool. Neil opened one eye as he heard the swimmer pass by him, and saw a large man swimming unrhythmically, arms clawing at the water clumsily, chunky legs splashing water violently into the air. He closed his eyes again and heard the swimmer clambering out of the pool, and sounding like he'd tripped over a plastic chair. Neil shuffled slightly uncomfortably as he felt the man approaching, and sitting down noisily in the sun lounger next to him.

"Alright mate?"

Neil really had no urge to get into a conversation with this bloke, but didn't want to be rude either.

"Alright," he replied without opening his eyes.

"Are you, though?" the other man said.

This time Neil did open his eyes. To his horror, the other bloke wasn't lying on the lounger next to him, but was sat on the side of it, facing towards Neil. To make things worse, he was wearing only a tiny pair of Speedo-style swimming trunks which looked several sizes too small for him. The trunks were almost completely engulfed by the man's huge gut and fat thighs. Looking briefly at his face, Neil felt sure he recognised him from somewhere, but was too horrified by the rest of him that he couldn't concentrate long enough to figure out where from. He turned away.

"Reason I ask," the man continued, his cockney accent now clearer, "is that you don't look alright to me."

"I'm fine, thanks."

"No. I don't think you are, mate."

Neil turned to face the stranger again. "Look mate, I don't want to be rude, but... hang on... aren't you..."

"Aaaah, now the penny drops, eh?"

It had now dawned on Neil who he was talking to. It was obvious now he'd realised, but the circumstances, location and context had been enough to distract him.

"You're Jim Davidson, aren't you?"

"The very same, my friend. The very same."

Knowing who he was talking to didn't make the situation any less odd or uncomfortable. In fact, being in this situation with a minor celebrity made it even stranger.

"Well, what are you doing here?" Neil asked.

"What am I doing here? I live here, mate."

"What, in Ipswich?"

"In the hotel. I live in the hotel. Have done for years."

"You live here? I thought you were a cockney."

"Well, a cockney by birth, but people don't stay in the same place all their lives do they, sunshine?"

"But, why a hotel?"

"Are you kidding me? It's the life, this is mate. You've got room service, big comfy bed, decent restaurant, and best of all, these lovely pool and spa facilities." He gestured around them. "I mean, it's a little slice of heaven, this is."

As Davidson stretched his arms out, his trunks shifted to the side, allowing one of his balls to drop loose. He didn't seem to notice or to care. Neil didn't know whether to say anything or not. He didn't want to embarrass anyone, but thought it would be more embarrassing to ignore it.

"Erm... you've come loose, there."

Davidson looked down. "So I have. Happens all the time that."

He tucked himself back in, then stretched out on his side, lifting one leg up, to make a loose triangle out of his two legs. He kept facing towards Neil. Not just facing towards him, but actively staring at him, squinting slightly as though trying to figure him out. Neil felt deeply uncomfortable. He didn't like being stared at, especially by almost naked men of such bulk. And he wasn't a fan of Davidson's comedy at all. He'd read things about him being a bit of a sod all in all.

"I'm going to use the sauna," he said, getting up from his lounger. Davidson said nothing, and Neil looked back to see that he was still staring at him.

He settled down in the sauna, but kept his eye on the door. Within seconds he saw the big silhouette of Davidson's frame lurking outside. Neil wished he'd just gone back to his room rather than coming in here, as the door slowly opened and the racist comedian entered. Without hesitation, he pulled off his swimming trunks, nearly tripping over as he did so. He stretched them out between his two hands, and aimed them before pinging them against the far wall, where they landed with a wet slap.

"Love that sound," he said, plonking himself down right next to Neil, and leaning in.

"I've seen you," he said, conspiratorially. "I've seen you before."

"I've never been here before," Neil replied, averting his eyes from the blubbery mass of Davidson's belly, and the tiny willy hanging down over the sauna bench.

"No, I don't mean actually *you*. I mean people like you. Your sort."

"My sort? What's my sort?" Neil asked, taking offence.

"The jaded sort. The weary kind. I see you all come in here, night after night, day after day, all with that same expression on your face. The one that says *'where did I go wrong?'* Well, thing is, mate, I can help you."

"Help me? Help me with what?"

"I can help rediscover the love, mate. I can turn that grimace into a grin. Here, let me show you something."

Davidson leaned right back, and pulled his fat legs right back over his head, sticking his bare arse in the air just inches away from Neil's face.

"Jesus, what are doing, Davidson?"

"It's alright mate, just bear with me a second."

And he reached round, and pulled his arse cheeks wide apart, to reveal an inflamed, sore looking anus with a haemorrhoid the size of a mini doughnut hanging off it.

"See that?"

"Of course I fucking see it, it's right by my face."

"Fifteen years I've had that." He sat back up. "And you know what, I don't care. Not in the slightest. You know why?"

Neil shook his head.

"Because, I've found inner fulfilment. True, Zen-like inner peace. And you wanna know where I found it?"

"Where?"

"Right here."

"What, in Ipswich?"

"No, you wally. In this hotel. Or, to be more specific, through the door."

"What door?"

"Come with me," Davidson said, not even waiting to see if Neil did follow him as he walked, naked as the day he was born, out of the sauna and along the side of the pool. He stopped and put an arm around Neil's shoulder and pointed towards a door off in the far corner. "You see that door? Inside that door, you'll find the answers to all the questions. You'll find out the true meaning of life. You'll go in as you are now, and come out a changed man, one so full of inner peace that every time you fart, the whole room will fucking reek of fulfilment."

Neil looked at the door. *'STAFF ONLY'* it said.

"It's just a door."

"No, it's not just a door. It's *THE* door, my old son. Now, the question is, do you wanna step through it with me, or do you wanna carry on walking around in a daze, like you have been the last Christ-knows how many years.?"

Neil shrugged Davidson's arm off his shoulder. "I don't know what you're talking about, I'm fine as I am. Now, if you'll excuse me, I've got meetings early in the morning."

"Of course you have, sunshine. But I'll be here when you get back, mate. I'll be waiting."

*

Neil pulled back into the Plaza Inn the next night, after an exhausting twelve-hour stint at a local logistics and trucking firm, trying to persuade them to update their photocopiers and computers to the latest range. After stringing him along all day, the finance director had ultimately kyboshed the idea. Neil was pissed off. Pissed off and humiliated. Stomping past the reception desk, he stopped. He looked towards the door that led to the pool area. Then he looked towards the bar. He decided on the bar, and ordered himself a double Bushmills. As the barman turned to get his drink, he looked back towards the door to the pool. Before his drink was even halfway dispensed, he was out of the bar, and walking straight into the pool. Sure enough, Davidson was sitting there, completely bollocko.

"I knew you'd be back."

"Yeah, alright. Don't rub it in. I'm back."

"You wanna see behind the door, me old son?"

"You know I do."

Davidson nodded. "Good. Very good. Let's go."

He put a fatherly arm around Neil's shoulder and guided him to the door.

"There you go, mate. Now, just knock three times, and all your troubles will be as forgotten as the sovereignty of this once-great nation."

"Are you not coming in?"

"No, mate. I've got all I need from in there. It's your turn now. I'll wait here."

Neil raised a tentative hand and knocked three times as instructed. The door opened slowly. Inside was only complete darkness. He turned back uncertainly to Davidson, who nodded his encouragement. Neil stepped inside, and the room became illuminated by a blinding light. Neil squinted as his eyes gradually adjusted. When he could finally see, stood in front of him was the young

Romanian from reception, wearing only a pair of tiny swimming trunks, and next to him, towering above them all, was a vast, hideous looking beast. It had chicken-like legs, but claws rather than wings, and instead of a beak, it had huge, yellow fangs, which were dripping with viscera. Terrified, Neil turned to run towards the door, but Davidson was already pushing it closed, his eyes on the ground.

"But Jim, you said you could help."

"I'm sorry, me old son," Davidson said, his eyes reluctantly meeting Neil's "It's the only way they'll let me keep living here. And I really like living here."

He looked back at the floor as he closed the door fully. Neil tried to open it, was it was locked from the other side. He put his back against it, and raised his hands in self-defence as the beast took a huge step towards him.

# Remember Me

*I was sitting on a bench at the end of the main shopping precinct when I decided to do it. Some ideas had been knocking around in my head for a while, but it was there that they really took shape. It's amazing how easily the biggest idea can come from nothing. There I was, just sitting watching the shoppers go by, and I'd just had an idea that would change my life, and change this town forever. I felt sorry for all these people now. All these fucking people who walk past me every day, ignoring me, looking through me, not even knowing I fucking exist. Well soon they'll know who I am. Nobody in this fucking town, in this fucking country, will ever forget me.*

\*

I get on the bus and tell the driver where I'm going. He looks straight ahead and says, "Two pound eighty."

No 'please'. No 'sir'. He drops the change into the little gutter thing. Just drops it for me to pick up myself. He can't just hand it to me, he has to throw it down. Then he starts pulling away while I'm stick picking the pennies up and I nearly fall over. I look at him and say 'hang on' but he doesn't even turn his head. He just keeps going and I have to stagger clumsily to my seat.

Two kids laugh at me struggling. I shoot them a nasty look. They just laugh even more. When the bus stops everyone just barges past each other trying to get off first. I see the kids who laughed at me push past an old woman as she tries to get off. Little fuckers. Little cunts.

I step off the bus and look around. It's too early for lunch yet so I decide to have a look round the shops. Just for something to do. I go into the big newsagents and have a look at the magazines. Sometimes I get lost in time flicking through those mags. I pick one up and before I know it, I've read the entire thing, cover to cover. I'm surprised they don't tell me to buy something or get out. Or tell me that this isn't a bloody library. I ask the fella behind the counter if the latest Radio Times is out yet.

"If it's out it's on the shelf," is all he says. Doesn't even look up from his own magazine. I stand there for a while to see if he'll say anything else. If he'll look up. He does neither, just keeps flicking over the pages of the mag he's reading. Bastard.

I walk out. I go to the cafe. I order myself a full English. Like I do every time I come in here, which is every other day. You'd think I wouldn't have to ask by now. A few months back I said 'the usual please, love' to the girl in there. Like you see people do on the telly and stuff. She looked at me like she'd never seen me before. Like I'd said something horrible to her. Fucking jumped up little tart. She works in a fucking greasy spoon and she thinks she can treat me like that. Like I don't matter. Like I'm nothing.

I walk to the supermarket for a few bits and pieces. Some bloke in the queue in front of me turns round and catches my eye. He looks away then quickly back again as though he recognises me, as though he's about to say something. But he doesn't. He just turns back and carries on queuing. A woman who works in the shop is rushing about getting another girl to open another till. She asks if anyone wants to come across to the other till and the fella who turned round and looked at me and the woman in front of him go over. I stay where I am. My queue isn't that long now they've moved.

"Sir. Would you like to come across please? Sir?"

It takes me a few seconds to realise the woman who was rushing about is talking to me.

"I'm okay," I say to her.

"We need to get the queues down sir, would you mind coming across please?"

I go across like she wants me to. I'm in no rush but it seems to mean a lot to her. Can't have her fucking queues being too long can we? The fucking world would end if she didn't get her queues down. Fucking miserable cow.

I get back on the bus to go home. It's a different driver to before, but it's the same treatment. Eyes forward, change chucked into the little gutter, nearly making me fall over by pulling away too quick. Fucking bus drivers. They're all the same.

I sit down to watch the telly while I eat my tea. The local news is on. The mayor is being interviewed at some public event. I've never seen him before. He's quite friendly, calling the reporter by his first name. He makes a bit of a joke. Not a joke. A pun, that's it. The interviewer laughs. I wonder if he would have laughed it he wasn't on camera. If it wasn't someone important like the mayor telling it. I wonder what he would have done if it had been me. If he would have laughed then. If he would have been acting all matey if the cameras were off. What would he do if I just went up to him and told him a joke, would he laugh with me? Would he fuck. He'd just think I was fucking nuts. Why? Why should the mayor be more important than me? Just because some people voted for him and he wears some stupid fucking medallion round his neck. He still pisses and shits the same as me.

The news report cuts to the mayor cutting a ribbon at some new building. Looks like some office block or something. Everyone is clapping and cheering.

The next time I go into town it's the same. Same miserable bus driver trying to make me fall over. Same snidey fucking tart in the greasy spoon. I try to make a bit of conversation with her, wondering if she'll be more receptive this time. Fat fucking chance. The little bitch doesn't even pretend to be interested in what I've got to say. Maybe if I jammed this fucking fork into her eye she'd be interested. She'd fucking notice me then.

I go to the newsagents again. I flick through the mags as usual. The same fella is behind the counter, leaning on it while he reads a magazine. I ask him when the next copy of a magazine is out.

"Next Thursday," he says, not looking up for a second.

"Look at me," I say, dead quietly. He either doesn't hear or doesn't listen.

"Look at me," I say a bit louder. This time he slowly looks up. He waits for me to do something. I must have a really angry face on because he looks a bit scared, like he thinks I'm going to hit him or something. I like the feeling that gives me. I just look at him for a few seconds then I walk out.

It's pissing down outside now. Everyone is rushing with their heads down, hoods or brollies pulled down to shield them from the wind and the rain. I walk along the main strip of the precinct. I have to keep moving out of the way of people who are looking down at the ground. It seems like everyone in the town is walking towards me. Like I'm the only one walking this way. Swimming against the tide. I'm sick of moving. Fuck them. Let them move for me. I walk in a straight line. People knock shoulders with me. Some say sorry, but most just keep going, not looking up for a second.

I start moving so that I'm barging into people now. Doing it deliberately. I'm nearly knocking some of them over. Every time I hit someone, I don't say sorry, I say "Look at me." But they don't. I barge into a few more people then I start getting out of breath from walking too hard, so I sit down on the bench. I sit and I watch everyone walking, heads down, stepping in puddles, knocking into each other, and it's right there, right then that I get the idea. Sitting on that bench in the pissing down rain it comes to me. Clear as day.

It takes weeks of looking through the local papers, looking online down at the library and watching the local news endlessly. Then I see my chance. My opening. There's no more planning needed. In fact, there wasn't that much for me to do at all. It's amazing really. The biggest thing I will ever do with my life. The biggest thing that will ever have happened in this town. And it took so little.

On the morning, I do everything I always do. I get the bus into town, but this time I've got the exact change ready. "Town," I say. No please, no thank you. I chuck the money down and walk to the back of the bus. I'm in my seat before he pulls away. I go into the newsagents. I pick up a magazine and put it under my jacket. I walk out without the fella even knowing I've been in there. I go into the cafe and order my full English. Of course, she doesn't look at me. But very soon she will realise she has just lived the most significant moment of her life. I eat my breakfast and read my stolen magazine. I look through the window and see the crowds already gathering. I don't rush. I wipe up the egg and bean juice with the last of my toast and drink the last of my tea. I leave the magazine on the table and walk outside.

I join the crowd and push my way to the front with one arm, the other hand gripping the knife handle tightly in my pocket. I'm at the front now, up against the barrier. I look down the road and can see the float. All the people on it are dressed in funny costumes, and the mayor is out in front, but coming over to the barrier shaking hands and high-fiving. Fucking man of the people. I try to put a fake smile on as I pull my hand halfway out my pocket. The mayor is right by me now. The music is deafening. It doesn't need to be this loud. He's right there now, right in front of me. He looks at me. Right fucking at me, and he thanks me for coming out, and he's passing by. My chance is passing me by, too. But before it's too late I lash out at him with the knife, but I don't do it like I mean to. It's not so much a stab, more of a slash, right across his neck. He just looks confused at first, like he doesn't know what's happened. Then his hand goes up to his neck and grabs his throat, and he starts to grit his teeth, and looks back to me. The blood is all coming through his fingers, so I know I must have done some damage. Someone screams in the crowd next to me, but she probably can't be heard over the sound of that bloody music. But then someone else screams, and another as they realise what's happened.

A copper is running over towards the mayor, pressing his hand against the mayor's neck and another one starts running over but trips. I turn round and the crowd all back away from me as they see the knife, I start to run but one man steps in front of me to try and stop me. I stab out at him with the knife and it sticks in his belly. Both his hands go towards the knife and I pull it out and I run past him and down the alleyway. I run round the corner to where the taxis all wait and jump into one. I keep the knife shoved into my pocket so the driver can't see any blood or anything and I tell him where I'm going. He tells me the parade has blocked up all the roads in the centre of town so he'll take a really long route round to avoid it all. When we get to my house, I give him a tenner with my clean hand and run into the house.

I switch the telly on and sit on the couch. I flick through a few channels till I find one with the news on. I watch as the newsreader is talking about something in another country, but they interrupt that and start talking about me. Well, they don't know they're talking about me yet, they just call it an 'incident' where the mayor has been stabbed. They say they will bring us more as they have it and go back to the other story so I run through some more channels.

Eventually I find one with more news about me. This news programme seems to know more. They've already got a reporter there talking to the camera. I can see the cafe behind her as she tells us that the mayor bled to death before an ambulance could even get to him. The other man who got stabbed at the scene is critical in hospital. I switch the telly off and I try and steady my breathing. My breathing slows and I lean back on the sofa. I pick up the pieces of paper I printed off at the library, all the stuff about John Bellingham, who killed Spencer Perceval. I get blood all over the pages so I can't read it, but I've memorised most of the facts about him by now. Him and Sam Byck. And John Hinkley Jr. They're not really famous names but they were a long time ago. Long before 24-hour news and the internet and all that, so I know I will be remembered much better. Nobody will forget me now.

I hardly slept last night, and I feel myself nodding off. I wake up an hour later. I pick up the phone and make the call, then I leave the house.

I walk the three miles into town. When I get to the police station, the news crew are waiting. They come running towards me when they see me. I'm holding the knife but I'm holding it up in a way that tells them I'm not going to use it any more, held high above my head.

The cameraman practically shoves the lens in my face. I don't mind though. I let him. I look straight into the camera. This is my moment. When the whole country, maybe even the whole world, will see me. The reporter is asking me my name and why I killed the mayor. I see the policemen running towards me with their guns pointed. Before they even tell me to do anything I throw the knife down and kneel on the floor. The reporter has been dragged away but the cameraman has got close again. I put my hands behind my head and stare into the lights and the cameras, all of them pointing at me.

# *Off Grid*

The man awakened to the sound of the child, who was making a low, anxious sound in his sleep. The man stood up from his mattress and walked over to him, placing his huge hand gently on the child's tiny, bony shoulder.

"Ssssssh, Michael. It's alright, son. You're okay. Dad's here."

He settled instantly. His father removed the hand from his shoulder and let him rest a short while longer. It was almost dawn now, so he'd be awake soon enough. Standing, he stepped towards the door of their cabin and gently opened it, stepping outside and breathing in the cool pre-dawn air. He turned back to look at his son, now probably ten years of age, though it was hard to know for sure. They kept track of the days as best they could, but could only estimate the date. He now gauged his son's age as much by his bodily growth as anything, and tracked his own age in relation to that.

Michael slept in the corner farthest from the door, his mattress on the floor, a large hunting knife on the floor next to it, a small pile of clothes folded neatly beside it. On top of the thin blanket was a small wooden toy his father had carved for him over a period of weeks from a single piece of firewood many months ago. It remained in the boy's bed, the one remaining concession to childhood.

He himself slept in the middle of the room, directly between his son and the door, fully dressed, his own hunting knife, even in deep sleep, clasped tightly in his left hand, his rifle loaded and within reach of his right.

He stepped back into the cabin and watched over his son as he slept, his beauty in sharp contrast to the horror of what his father had to protect him from. Again he began to murmur, and again a strong hand was placed onto his shoulder, but this time it shook him gently awake. He opened his eyes and gazed up.

"Dad," he said. It was not a question, nor an indication of surprise, but a simple reiteration of the one thing he knew for sure, the one thing he could rely on. He reached up and placed his hands around his father's neck, pulling him in close. They kissed each other on the cheek, and the boy let go, rubbing the last of the sleepiness from his eyes.

"Are we going out?" he asked, sitting up and reaching for his clothes.

"We are. Let's go and find some breakfast."

"Can I do it today?" Michael asked.

The man nodded and smiled. "Get your knife."

*

The man watched on, sharpening their knives against a rock, as the child carefully laid the snare trap as he had been taught many times.

"Good work," he said when the trap was ready. "Now, let's go and wash."

Together they walked down to the stream. Naked, they stood in the freezing water, washing as the rapid water crashed noisily around them. He looked at his son; still skinny, but with muscles beginning to develop across his chest and upper arms, growing out of the daily hard work that a boy of his age shouldn't have to experience. The man looked down at his own body; the muscles large and taut, his hands grown huge and calloused from the life he now lived, one a million miles away from his previous life. The life he lived before the world changed, leaving him no choice but to change with it.

When they had cleaned themselves, they cleaned the pile of clothes they had brought with them, holding the garments against the flow of the water, rubbing them against each other, then whipping them against a large rock to remove the excess water. As the man shook out a pair of trousers, he felt something slap hard against the side of his face. He looked down to see a wet sock lying on the rock, and looked back up to see Michael grinning at him. The man raised an eyebrow, and quickly hurled a wet shirt of his own in his son's direction. It landed with a satisfying slap against his chest. The child chased him around the rocks, throwing item after item of sodden clothing at him.

*

After they'd hung the clothes up to dry outside the cabin, they walked back to the trap. A rabbit hung upside down in the snare, its legs twitching and kicking violently.

"It's a big one," Michael said, trying to contain his pride.

"It is," said his father, putting his arm round his shoulder. "Well done."

"Thank you."

"Okay. You'll have to finish it off now."

The child took a deep breath and nodded his head, and without hesitation, stepped forward and did what needed to be done.

\*

"Remember," the man said, back at the cabin, "you only need a small cut with the knife, then you can just rip most of the skin off with your hands."

He sat and watched as Michael made a small incision with his knife, before sticking both index fingers inside, ripping the skin down the middle, and peeling it back and down. The skin became stuck halfway down, leaving the carcass with the unbefitting absurd look of a skinny man with his shirt stuck over his head, and he became frustrated that he was unable to remove the skin in one go.

"That's okay. If it gets stuck, just stick the tip of your knife back in and make another little cut."

He did as instructed, and was able to pull the skin the rest of the way down, where it again became stuck at the animal's feet and head. This time, he wasn't frustrated, he just took his knife back out, and cut off the feet, followed by its head. He threw the skin to one side, knowing it could be utilised, and placed the carcass onto the stump of a tree which often doubled as a table or seat, and began to butcher the animal with a skill far beyond his years. While he did this, the man walked to the far side of the clearing where they had built their cabin, and picked some wild mushrooms, burdock and purslane.

"We'll cook outside, shall we?" the man asked.

The child looked back over his shoulder, smiled and nodded.

*

Later, they walked south of their cabin, the man carrying his rifle slung over his shoulder, his knife in a holster around his waist, a hatchet hanging from his belt. The only sound to be heard was the sound of their feet falling softly against leaves and twigs. But in an instant, each of them stopped dead, and turned their ears towards the same thing.

"Dad," Michael whispered, "what..."

His voice trailed off. He didn't need to complete the question. They both knew what they were hearing. Though distant, the sound was unmistakable. The child had seldom heard it, but could identify it easily. It was the sound of an engine, a bike engine. More than one, in fact.

"Run," the man said, grabbing his son's hand.

They sprinted up the hill and along the top of it, into an area thick with bushes. They dropped onto their bellies and crawled to the edge, where they were still well hidden, but had a view of the area below and ahead of them. He took out his rifle and looked through its sight. In it he saw, twenty feet down and five hundred yards away, two small bikes coming to a halt. The riders stepped off their bikes to investigate. They kicked at the huge log that blocked the track they'd been on.

"I thought we blocked the paths off lower down," the child said, still whispering in fear of his voice carrying on the wind.

"We did," the man replied.

They watched as one of the riders took off his helmet. The man could see through his rifle that he was young, maybe seventeen years old. He could feel the vibrations of his son's heart pounding against the ground. He spoke quietly to reassure the child, but realised it was in fact his own heart pounding.

"What are they, Dad? Scavengers?"

"Maybe."

He froze as the rider without his helmet looked in their direction and stopped, his face pointing right at them. The boy saw it too.

"Does he see us, Dad?"

"I don't think so. But don't worry. Even if he does, I see him. I've got him in my sights. If he takes another step towards us I'll take his head off his shoulders."

The rider looked away and went back to conversing with the other. For a few minutes more they stood there, passing something back and forth to each other, something they were eating, or perhaps smoking. Eventually, they shrugged and mounted their bikes, revving the engines before moving off. The rider at the back, the one who had removed his helmet, turned back briefly in their direction before he disappeared from site. Even after they had vanished and the sound had dissipated, the man kept his rifle aimed in their direction.

"Will you give me some more lessons with my rifle, Dad?"

"We'll start again in the morning," he nodded.

*

That night he put his son to bed. When he was sure he was sound asleep, he left the cabin, locking it from the outside, knowing Michael would signal as they had practiced if needs be. He walked out behind the cabin, the side they rarely accessed, and walked up through the thick trees, forcing his way through the jungle-like bush and out into the clearing where he had been only once before, and where the child had not yet trod. He looked out through his rifle sight at the distant monstrosity; the tall buildings billowing smoke and chemicals, the vast structure of glass and steel, the freeway with its metal animals scurrying around upon it.

"Civilisation," he said to himself.

He squeezed the trigger, and fired into the distance.

# He Goes Again

'One of the most naturally gifted midfielders of his generation.'

'Possesses a vision and passing range unseen in British football for decades.'

'Has the ability and the temperament to go all the way to the very top.'

Michael Carey had grown accustomed to such praise. Spotted as a likely future great early on in his development at the club's academy, he'd been spoken of in enthusiastic terms since his early teens. Since signing a five year professional contract at eighteen, he'd kept his head down, listened to his coaches, learned from the older pro's and, now at twenty two, had just signed a new four year deal with the club he'd played for all his life, resisting the temptation of the big European clubs, and had recently made his debut for England, creating a goal and several other opportunities with his clever passing and movement.

In that same game, however, he'd also picked up an injury to his calf. Nothing serious, but one that was likely to keep him out of action for between two and four weeks. As was typical of the lad, he'd taken the news philosophically, and gone about his physio work with the same relish he approached training and competitive matches. Lying on his front on the physio's table, he was now getting a rub down from Baz, a long-serving member of the club's medical staff.

"How are you feeling then, lad?" Baz asked him.

"Pretty good, thanks Baz. I reckon another week of treatment and I'll be back in full training."

"That's good news. Just don't push yourself, son, that's all. No point aggravating a minor injury, is there?"

"No, no way, mate. I'll be fine."

"Good lad. If I had a pound for every minor muscle strain that's been turned into a muscle tear by players rushing themselves back, well, I wouldn't have to work here anymore, that's for sure."

Baz and Michael laughed together, even though they both knew Baz had used that same line a hundred times before. Baz's laughter halted abruptly, though, as his hands moved down to the back of Michael's calf.

"Aye, aye," he said, "what's this, then?"

"What's what, mate?"

"This, here on the back of your leg. There's something there, like... a scab or something?"

"A scab? Let's have a look at it."

Michael turned onto his back and lifted his leg up, angling his head so he could get a proper look at it. He reached down and prodded it.

"That's bit fucking weird, like," he said.

And he was right, it was a bit weird. Roughly the size of a two pence coin, hard and scaly to the touch. He pulled at it gently.

"Does it hurt?" Baz asked him.

"No. Not really."

"Does it come off?"

"I don't think so. It's like it's part of the skin."

Baz scratched his head. "Hmmm, I think we'd better get the club doctor to have a look at it, mate. Could be some kind of skin condition."

"No," Michael said, raising a reassuring hand. "Tell you what, just let me get home today and rest up, and we'll see what it's like tomorrow, okay? If it's still there then we'll speak to the doc. Okay?"

"Yeah, alright," Baz agreed reluctantly. "But do rest up today, okay? Don't be exerting yourself or owt like that, right lad?"

"Yeah, no worries. I'll be back in the morning."

Michael jumped into his BMW, stopped to sign some autographs for the kids waiting at the training ground gates, and sped home, where he went straight to bed.

*

The next morning, he headed straight to the treatment room to see Baz.

"How is it, lad?" Baz asked him before he'd even had the chance to say good morning

"Well, not too good to be honest, mate."

Michael lifted up his trouser leg to reveal two more of the scaly lesions next to the first one.

"Oh, shite."

"Yeah, but that's not all, Baz."

He took his top off and turned around to show another four on his back, as well as two on the underside of his left bicep, and one on his right flank.

"Right. We'll have to get the gaffer and the doctor to see this, son."

103

*

In the doctor's office, Michael lay on his back, stripped down to his underpants, as Dr. Megson examined him, and his manager, Eddie, paced the office anxiously.

"Well," Eddie shouted. "What the fucking hell are they?"

Megson took his glasses off and sighed. "Scales," he said, shaking his head.

"What? Fucking scales? What the fucking hell you on about, scales?"

"Scales?" Michael repeated, sounding more afraid than angry.

"That's what they look like to me, gentlemen."

"Why the fucking hell have you got fucking scales growing out of your fucking legs, you little shit?" Eddie yelled in Michael's face.

"I dunno, boss. Honest."

"What the hell have you been up to, boy? Who the fucking hell have you been hanging round with?"

"Nothing, boss. No one, honest."

Eddie turned back to the doctor. "Why the fucking hell has he got fucking scales growing out of his fucking arms and legs, you fucking quack? What fucking shite having you been giving him, eh? Pills or fucking injections?"

Megson held his hands up. "I haven't given him a thing, I assure you."

"You'd better fucking not have. So why's he got them, then, you fucking overpaid Harley Street smart arse? And will he be able to get back to training next week?"

"At this point, I really can't answer either of those questions," Megson said as he picked up the phone on his desk and began dialling. "I think they'll have to run some tests."

*

"Okay, we need to strategize here, people."

Alan Doyle, the club's director of communications was holding the floor, as Michael, Eddie, Dr. Megson and C.E.O. John Hill sat and listened.

"We can keep a lid on this for, at best, twenty four hours, okay? After that, this is gonna break somehow. Probably on Twitter first, then in the papers. It only takes one person to leak it, then we're looking at a river of information we can't dam."

"Dams don't stop rivers, you daft fucking college boy twat," shouted Eddie.

"Alright, Eddie. Just calm down. So what do we do?" Hill asked.

"Well, if we accept there's no way to stop this breaking, the best we can do is control the flow of information as early as possible, and to own the narrative here. For starters I'll draft a statement –"

"A fucking statement? Saying what, for fuck's sake? Saying that my best player has got fucking lizard DNA? People will think it's a fucking joke."

Alan held his hands up to placate Eddie.

"Eddie," he said, "what we do is we play down the lizard aspect, and we focus on difference. We focus on the fact that Michael has a difference, but that he's still human. Erm, you are still human, right Michael?"

Michael shrugged his shoulders. "Erm, I think so. Doc?"

Megson gave a shrug of his own. "As far as I'm aware. I must emphasise, however, that this is the first case of its kind I've ever heard of."

"Okay, so we say he's still human, just different. We make a plea for tolerance, and acceptance. That's how we spin it."

"You spin it any way you like, flash boy. Fact of the matter is my best passer has got fucking lizard scales coming out of his fucking arsehole. It's a fucking farce."

Eddie stormed out of the office, slamming the door behind him.

*

Twelve hours later, the club released a statement on its website and social media, explaining that the club had recently become aware that Michael Carey possessed an as-yet-unspecified amount of lizard DNA. The club asked that Michael be treated with dignity and respect. He was after all, just a young man who simply wanted to be allowed to continue to ply his trade to the best of his considerable capabilities. For Michael's part, the club said, he would be issuing no separate statement at this time, as he simply wished to let his football do the talking.

Unsurprisingly, Twitter instantly exploded. Gifs, memes and banter prevailed, in amongst some genuine nuanced debate about whether a man with scales should be allowed to continue to play professional football. Many pointed out that nowhere in the rules of association football is it stated that players must be human, and many pointed out that it was as yet unclear as to whether Michael could no longer be classed as human.

With Michael still recovering from his injury, his team played their next match under his shadow. Opposing fans chanted *"Where's your lizard gone? Where's your lizard gone?"* to which Michael's club's support responded with *"He may be a lizard, but he's ours"* and *"One Michael Carey, there's only one Michael Carey."*

A week later, in another home game, Michael made his return to the starting line-up, in a match broadcast live on Sky Sports. All eyes were on the young English midfielder, and he didn't disappoint. His passing was quick, positive and precise, as people had come to expect of him. He was dynamic and energetic, tracking back to make several crucial interceptions, and his set piece delivery was consistently excellent; the game's only goal resulting from a viciously whipped in free-kick, which was glanced home by the head of centre-back and captain Billy Harper, who instantly ran to Michael to celebrate with him, as did the rest of the team.

Michael was awarded the man-of-the-match award, which he accepted on-camera with typical humility.

"It's not about me, it's about the team, and I'm just glad I've been able to contribute to a vital win today," he said, shutting the interview down quickly but politely before any questions could be asked about the scales which were now visible down his arms, on the back of one hand, and above the sock and shin-pad on his left leg.

The pundits in the studio were effusive in their praise for him, and when the anchor brought up the lizard in the room, Gary Neville leaped to his defence.

"Look," he said, "all that matters, at the end of the day, is whether he's good enough to play the game, and today has shown he is. We've seen this kind of performance time and again from this lad. And as for all the other stuff that's being said on social media about him, all I'll say is this; we've been waiting for this type of player for years, now you wanna tear him down because he's got some lizard DNA? Just leave the lad to play his game."

Not all pundits were as supportive, though. The next morning, Neil Warnock appeared on Sunday Supplement, having been the manager on the receiving end of Michael's talents the previous day, and, when asked about Carey, he didn't hold back.

"Well, I think it's a bit of a disgrace to be honest. I mean, back when I played you wouldn't have had this. When I was at York or Hartlepool, if a player had come into the dressing room covered in scales or wot-not, I don't think he'd have been made very welcome, quite frankly."

The social media response to Warnock's comments was mixed. Many ex-pros echoed his statements, with Ian Wright and Rodney Marsh saying they'd have been uncomfortable. Sam Allardyce appeared yet again alongside Richard Keys and Andy Gray.

"Well, this is just the way things seem to be going now, not just in football but in the country as a whole. Next well be getting told we have to select players from other planets."

Joey Barton stated his support for Carey during an interview with 5 Live, as did Pat Nevin, who interrupted his DJ slot at All Tomorrow's Parties in Iceland to tell the crowd *'Anyone with the ability to play the game should be allowed to do so without persecution'.*

The Secret Footballer tweeted a link to a blog post where he claimed, in every dressing room he'd ever been in that Carey wouldn't necessarily be welcome, but he would be accepted and eventually supported as long as he kept performing on the pitch. Jamie Rednapp, on the other hand, was only able to muster a confused shrug when asked for his take.

By Monday morning, the issue had gone far beyond the world of football. Owen Jones penned a piece for The Guardian about how Carey must be supported by all, both inside and outside the football world, as *'the issue of how we treat our lizard brothers and sisters could become a defining issue of our age, and if we alienate Carey and his kind now, we will find ourselves on the wrong side of history.'* When questioned on what he meant by 'Carey and his kind', given that Carey's was the only case of its kind being discussed, Jones went on a Twitter blocking spree and made his account private, but not before tweeting that *'Those persecuting Michael Carey today are the same people who would have spat at Cyril Regis thirty or forty years ago.'*

Through all of this, perhaps the only person not talking about Michael Carey was Michael Carey himself, who had kept a dignified public silence. But now he was back on the treatment table, with Baz, Eddie, Alan Doyle, John Hill and Dr. Megson all crammed into the room.

"Show us then, lad," Baz said reassuringly.

Michael rolled onto his front and pulled his shorts halfway down his backside. Everyone's eyes were initially drawn to the scales that now covered and pointed to the base of his spine.

"Here," he said, "I noticed it last night, but it seems a bit bigger this morning."

Megson prodded at the lump, the size and texture of a sweet potato, jutting out and threatening to break out of the skin.

"Some... sort of... erm... boney protrusion of some sort..." he mumbled uncertainly.

"Boney protrusion?" Eddie shouted at him. "Stop mincing your fucking words, doc. It's a fucking tail, ain't it? The lad's growing a fucking tail!"

"Well, yes, that's certainly a possibility."

Eddie turned to Alan. "How the fucking hell are you gonna fucking spin this one then, dickhead?"

Alan began to raise his phone to his ear, but stopped halfway, shook his head, and left the room without a word.

"Can I still play this weekend, boss?" Michael asked pleadingly. "I feel fine."

"Fine? You're covered in fucking scales, boy. And you won't be feeling too fucking fine when you give a penalty away when some fucker decides to take a dive over your fucking tail!"

*

Whether Michael would be able for selection the following weekend was now no longer a matter for him, Eddie, or the club. In an interview given by Jose Mourinho, whose Manchester United team would be the next opponents; Mourinho questioned whether Michael's condition counted as gaining an unfair advantage, in the same way the use of performance enhancing drugs did.

"For instance," Jose had said, "does it give him greater agility? This tail he is apparently now growing, this may provide him with greater balance, and possibly give him a stronger jump from dead-ball situations. I don't know, I'm not a doctor or a vet, but it seems to me like this player has an unfair advantage."

Mourinho made it clear United would submit a complaint if Michael so much as appeared on the pitch, even if his team won.

This had prompted the F.A. to act. Representatives visited the club, speaking with Michael and the club's hierarchy. FIFA also sent a delegate to investigate. After several hours of discussion, the decision was made by the F.A. to temporarily suspend Michael from the game, pending further investigations and consultations. The club were outraged, and their lawyers threatened to sue, stressing the fact that nowhere in either F.A. or FIFA rules does it state that a player must be fully human.

Michael, though, had been worn down by the entire affair, and accepted the decision. A day later, he called a press conference at the club's training ground, during which, flanked by Eddie and John Hill, he announced his retirement from the game, with immediate effect.

"I'd like to place on record," he said, reading from a prepared statement, "my gratitude to the club, the staff and, most of all, the fans. The support I've received, not only in recent weeks, but during my entire time here, has been incredible, and I'll never forget it. I'd also like to acknowledge the support I've received from the wider footballing community. I feel this is the right course of action, and I'd be grateful if everyone could now respect my privacy, as I learn to come to terms with what has transpired recently. Thank you."

He stood up and, without taking any questions, left the room, knocking a jug of water off the table with his tail as he did so.

"Fucking hell," one journalist sad to another, "this is better than when Cantona retired."

"I know," said the other. "I mean, Cantona didn't have a fucking tail for starters, did he?"

*

After that press conference, Michael Carey was not seen in public again. Some speculated that he'd moved to a commune for similarly afflicted people somewhere in Mexico. Some claimed he moved back in with his parents, but nobody could find any strong evidence to support either theory. So Michael Carey became another footballing recluse, to be spoken about in pubs and on forums, compared in blog posts and articles to Peter Wilson and Peter Knowles as one of the sport's great, enigmatic disappearing acts, and remains, to this day, Britain's only professional footballer with lizard DNA.

Printed in Great Britain
by Amazon